Millie's China

by

Edie Lambert

Promise Publishing Co. Orange, California 92865

Millie's China

Printed in the United States of America

Copyright 1998 by Promise Publishing Co.

Orange, California 92865

Library of Congress Cataloging-in-Data

Lambert, Edie

Millie's China

ISBN 0-939497-48-4

Table of Contents

Chapter One

MILLIE'S EARLY YEARS IN CHINA

My sister, Millie, and I were traveling on a train in far Southwest China, going from Xichang to Kunming. It was 1986 and I was part of a tour group that Millie took to an area of China that had been closed to outsiders for many years.

Mother and Papa had opened a station in Xichang (formerly Sichang) when they were young missionaries. Now, some of their fellow missionaries who had been expelled many years before, were returning. Those dark days ended with harrowing trips down the Yangtse River, imprisonment and house arrest for the missionaries - even the death of one mother of five. Millie and I were among the missionary kids born in Western China who made up the rest of our tour group - about twenty in all. We had waited nearly a lifetime to make a return visit.

In those early days, the missionaries had come to Xichang by way of the Yangtse River, by animals and by foot to reach this outpost of missionary work. Now, as a grandmother, I was returning on a train with these few others who had also called this area "home" in years gone by.

As China began to open to outsiders, Millie began visiting deeper and deeper into the country to contact the many friends she had made through her years of exile from the mainland. Now we were permitted to travel to this distant part of China's interior. We travelled in compartments with four bunks and a tiny eating area for the the five days and nights it took to make our way through the foothills of the Himalayas. We crossed countless trestles and passed through many long tunnels. The hills were still barren where the government had stripped the red mountains of their trees to prevent their enemies from hiding in the rugged forests that had stood there. The rivers ran red with mud from the mountains.

As we neared Kunming, the terrain changed and we found ourselves in a humid, tropical setting with hills covered in lush greenery. We were impressed with the Stone Forest, just outside Kunming, with its strange black cliffs where streams seemed to gush past at every turn. It was late Saturday afternoon as we neared the city.

I asked Millie, "Have you ever been out here in Kunming before?"

"No, not way down here," she replied. "We're almost in Vietnam!"

"Oh," I said, "then you don't know anyone in Kunming."

"Well, that's not exactly true," she answered, "I've been writing to a Bible woman here - the mother of a girl I met in Hong Kong." The Bible woman lived in Kunming - nearly all the way across China, and neither she nor her daughter had been able to secure permission to visit the other. "She might meet us at the train depot," Millie offered.

Sure enough, when the train pulled into the station, the Bible woman was there with several friends and relatives she wanted Millie to meet. She recognized Millie at once and immediately started thanking her for being such a good friend to her daughter so far away in Hong Kong. I shouldn't have been surprised. Millie seemed to know *someone* in every province in China, even though the Communist government hadn't allowed her to live in China for more than thirty years!

Millie introduced the Bible woman to one of our tour group, John Simpson, who had been a missionary with the China Inland Mission and had served with some of the tribes people west of Kunming before the Second World War. The Bible woman was now working with some of the same people! She talked with us animatedly all evening about the little home gatherings and the people in them. It was wonderful to hear how she continued the work that he started so very many years before.

The next morning, the Bible woman met us at the now open services of the Kunming Protestant Church, and introduced our tour group (especially Millie) to the pastors. They were very welcoming. The former Presbyterian pastor told us that while he had been detained by the Communist government, his mother had come daily to the front of the closed church, and prayed that some day it would be open again. How happy his mother now was to see her prayers answered, the church open, her son freed and again established as pastor of the church. We thanked God, too, as we joyfully worshipped Jesus together in their full church.

After church, Millie gave extra Bibles to her new pastor friends and the Bible woman, and promised to write and visit them again. We were soon on the train, making our way to the next stop where Millie knew someone else.

That was my sister Millie. She spent her life first living *in* China, then writing letters *to* China, *visiting* folks in China, or *trying to get back* into China to find more of her friends! I must admit that Millie had a head start in knowing about the Orient since our parents were missionaries and we were both born in West China.

Millie's First Letter

Millie's birthdate was October 15, 1919. One of the fun things she received when she was only three months old was a letter from Emanuel Schmidt, Ph.D., a professor of Hebrew at Bethel Theological Seminary.

The address on the envelope said simply:

Miss Mildred Effie Lovegren

Yachow, Szechwan, China

I'm surprised she received it since it had no house numbers or street address - not a box number, mission, nor anything to tell what section of the city she was in. Yachow *was and is* a city, not a small town. Amazingly, it only cost five cents to send! Her sparsely addressed letter said:

St. Paul, Minn.

January 16, 1920

My dear little friend:

Although I have not yet had the pleasure of seeing you, I trust your fond parents' report about you is correct, weight 7-3/4 pounds, length 21-1/2 inches. I presume by the time this letter reaches you, these measures shall have changed considerably.

Well, I welcome you to this world of ours. You are very fortunate in having found such a house, for I know your parents well, and can assure you that you have made a good choice. I congratulate you for arriving in such a wonderful empire. You will no doubt see your fatherland advance to one of the most important countries of the world, as it is one of the most populous.

May you grow strong and healthy and become a source of real joy to your parents. Give them my best regards by singing for them a real lullaby in unadulterated Chinese.

Your friend,

E. Schmidt

Safe in the Compound

As young missionary children, we played *and stayed* inside the walls of the missionary compound. There were fewer dangers there. Chinese people liked to touch the light, blond tots. They were just curious and friendly, **but** did they have dysentery (the disease that killed our older sister, Anna Louise), or cholera, or maybe even leprosy?

Inside the compound there were two houses that were two or three stories high, with wide porches surrounding the upper floors. The rooms were large and airy, well built of of wood and heated by fireplaces made of brick. From the second story verandas, the children could see over the five-foot wall to the Chinese world outside their gate. The Yangtse River flowed nearby and the city stretched out before them. There was a Giant Buddha not far away.

We could see the Yangtse River from our balcony

Millie, Edie and Norman at our childhood home in Western China

Our old house was still there when we went to visit

Millie was allowed to go with the folks to the Chinese Church
and play with the other children during Sunday School and after
the services. She even went very briefly to a Chinese kindergarten
before our first furlough, but usually she only played with other
missionary children inside the compound.

These were the missionaries on the compound in those days

Mother and Papa with Millie and August

The compound was its own little world. We drank the water from the river beside the compound after it had gone through Papa's extensive filtering system. Papa had constructed an elaborate set of barrels filled with rocks and sand to purify the abundant water supply.

Papa kept two or three cows to provide milk for the missionary families. We had a "cow man" to care for them who lived in his own house away from the compound, coming in every day to do his job. Papa carefully taught him to graze the cows in the fields, wash them carefully before milking, and also to wash his hands and the pails. I imagine that the milk was also boiled. The cows were pastured outside the compound, but at night, they were always kept inside.

We had at least one pet dog, a pointer, who was not only our pet, but a watchdog as well. If nothing else looked like fun, Millie was fascinated by the little frogs. She would search them out and stamp her foot, or use a twig to make them jump. Millie thought that was great fun.

In Kiating, there was a little gateman's house and two large houses making up the compound - the Lovegren House and the Jensen House, named for the largest of the families that lived in them. The middle floor of the Lovegren House was where we lived. Our favorite "uncle", Harry Oppenshaw, a single missionary, lived above us.

Harry J. Openshaw, Millie, Norman and August

There were other missionaries living below us at different times, and many guest rooms. This was one of the features of every missionary home. They all had guest bedrooms with clean sheets, blankets, and towels. Missionaries in these far reaches of Western China were always expected to have extra food on hand, not only for missionary guests, but also for foreign travelers when they needed a safe, clean place to spend the night. It was almost like running a hotel, but luckily for the missionaries, there were servants to do most of the housework. The missionaries needed freedom to do the work of the Gospel, and the Chinese needed the income.

The Chinese servants with Papa and another missionary

August on the primitive, swinging bridge

One of the very nice things about this arrangement was that missionaries got acquainted with each other and were a lot less lonely in a foreign country. When a missionary needed to stay, there was always room. For instance, when I was born, the nearest American doctor and nurse were in Yachow, almost a full day's journey from Kiating. As the time drew near, Papa took mother and brother, Norman, to Yachow to stay at the compound near Dr. R.L. Crook and nurse, Ada Nelson. We were welcome to stay as long as we wished.

Our hometown, Kiating, was a city that tourists wanted to see even though getting there was a long, hard journey. A giant Buddha had been carved in the mountain where two tributaries of the mighty Yangtse River met. The Buddha was "protection" for boats that were trying to navigate the turbulent waters there. It was so large that four or five people could stand on an individual toe. We could easily see the great Buddha from our compound just up the river. Among the diplomats, tourists, and explorers that stayed at our house were President Teddy Roosevelt and sons, Teddy and Kermit. Their party was looking for Giant Pandas and for the 24,000 foot mountain, Minya Gongga, west of us.

This "open house" policy was one that Millie followed all of her life. Her house was always open to friends, relatives, and visitors. She also expected other missionaries to have the gift of hospitality; in fact, this was true not only on the mission field, but also in the United States. She invited many people to our house whenever she was staying with us.

> "Do not neglect to show hospitality to strangers, for thereby some have entertained angels unawares" (Hebrews 13:2).

They Never Gave Me Paper Dolls

It takes a certain type of person to become a missionary - not only one who loves Jesus and wants to serve Him, but also someone who is adventurous, strong-willed, and independent. These "talents" are needed if missionaries are going to be able to endure hardships, cultural differences, new languages, and changing circumstances. Of course, just because these people have been mainly Westerners trying to serve God in a foreign place, doesn't mean that they all agreed on how this should be done. In fact, strong-willed people *often* don't agree. With sadness and some shock, Millie discovered this fact early in life.

When she was only six, she admired a lady missionary who was kind to her and gave her some paper dolls. She thought this missionary was marvelous. The lady had already lived through some hard circumstances, the worst being the loss of her husband during their first term of service. Most widows would have returned to America immediately, but she determinedly stayed on in China trying to fulfill their call from God.

At a mission meeting with our parents, where our group of missionaries had come to discuss their problems and successes, Millie overheard two of them criticizing her widow lady. They felt she was very set in her ideas and hard to live with. Millie felt the talkers were wrong, and she thought to herself, "Why are they talking about her? *They* never gave me any paper dolls!" In fact, no one else had!

Many times as Millie grew up, it would hurt her when she heard Christians criticizing others. She would think about her paper dolls and feel that no one is able to really know what kindnesses each person has done, or how God judges our actions and words. She often found that people who influenced her life and ministry the most were independent enough to receive at least some opposition from fellow missionaries.

Did Millie ever give paper dolls? Yes! I have no idea how many, but I know of one little girl in Sri Lanka who wrote to thank "Aunt Millie", and there was a mother in India who also appreciated the coloring book and paper dolls that her little daughter received.

Mother had a plaque on my bedroom wall that I did not particularly like, but I inadvertently memorized:

> "There is so much bad in the best of us,
>   And so much good in the worst of us,
> That it little behooves any of us,
>   To talk about the rest of us."

Shanghai

Furlough time! This is a wonderful time when missionaries return to the United States to see relatives and friends, to rest, to get newly inspired, and to talk to the sponsoring churches. Sometimes it was an upsetting time for us children. Just think - a year of always traveling and trying to be good so far away from our Chinese home. We started the first long leg of our journey with days and nights aboard a ship, making our way down the Yangtse River to Shanghai. Then we had a few days to rest before taking the steamer across the Pacific.

Millie's earliest remembered experience in Shanghai was not a happy one, but it was one that she was later glad she had, because it influenced her behavior from then on. Our family was in Shanghai waiting to board the steamer that would take them back to America for their first furlough. Millie got to go shopping with the folks. At one counter, just at eye level, Millie saw some brightly colored toy balloons and decided she wanted one. She reached up, took a balloon, and put it in her pocket. They had left the store and gone about a block when Millie decided to blow up the balloon. At first, the folks were busy talking and didn't notice what Millie was doing, but as the balloon got larger, Mother looked down and asked where she had gotten it. Millie said rather vaguely that it was from the store. Soon Papa was asking, too; both parents were sharply questioning her. It wasn't until she got badly scolded that she had any feelings of guilt. They marched Millie back to the store, one on each side, and made her tell the salesgirl that she had taken it. It was terrible! Later Millie was glad that she was taught honesty so easily. Stealing was never again a temptation in her life.

After furlough, the family went all the way back to West China, but they weren't able to stay long. The Communist band called the Red Bandits were marching south through Szechwan Province. War lords were also viciously fighting each other. The American Consul ordered the missionaries to return to Shanghai for their safety. The family had to leave immediately. Millie remembered a rather exciting trip down the Yangtse River.

Once or twice they had to get up in the middle of the night to go to the bridge of the ship for safety against armed attacks. Still, the only time she actually saw any Communists was one morning while they were going through the river gorges. There were several hundred men along the shore, dressed in red and carrying large red banners. The marines on board their river steamer were prepared for an attack, but the Red Bandits did not fire on the ship.

When the family arrived in Shanghai, they went to live at Shanghai College, an American Baptist school where Papa taught for about eight months. Later, Papa was able to return to West China, but the family stayed in Shanghai for another nine months until it was deemed safe for a family to travel.

Millie liked living in Shanghai. There were a large number of children who had a Chinese background similar to her own. They were of different nationalities, but all spoke English well. She went to most of first and second grade on the campus there in Shanghai. She learned to swim. Stuffed with pillows, she took part in a circus as the fat lady. It was fun.

Our family in Shanghai

The birthday party

After Papa went back West, the family moved from the college campus to the French settlement in Shanghai. Their house was next door to the gardens and home of F.V. Sung, China's financier who later became President of China and whose brother-in-law was Generalissimo Chiang Kai-shek. The Sungs had two boys and one girl. The boys were about the ages of

August and Norman, five and three, and the girl was older than Millie who was seven.

Millie and her brothers squirmed through a small hole in the wall of the French compound and through a hedge, and introduced themselves to the Sung children. They seemed delighted. They weren't allowed to have many friends for fear of kidnapping. They also spoke English, which was wonderful because the Shanghai dialect of Mandarin was hard for our family to understand. *And* the Sung children had all kinds of pets and games! Millie and her brothers had a wonderful time playing with these important children for the nine months they lived in the French settlement.

After that, our family always followed the victories and trials of this leading Sung family and the Chiang family, as one does close personal friends because, for a brief while, our children were pals with their children.

Boarding School

By the time Millie was ready for the third grade, the family was at home again in Kiating near Tibet in West China. There was no school for missionary children in Kiating. For a little while, Mother taught both Millie and August; however, Papa and Mother soon decided that Millie needed to go to a regular school. The closest mission school was in Chengtu only one day's journey by bus, and the school would provide room and board for her. Millie absolutely *refused to go!*

Finally, Papa and Mother reached a compromise with Millie; they would send little brother August to school with her, so she wouldn't be lonely. Millie reluctantly agreed. Good natured little August didn't mind.

It was the summer of 1928 when Millie was almost nine and August was six-and-a-half that these two older children left Kiating with Papa by bus for the all-day, one-hundred-mile journey to the Canadian School for missionary children in

Chengtu. As they drove along on rough dirt roads, they passed many fields that were literally covered with gorgeous flowers of varied colors. Millie thought they were tulips, but Papa explained that they were poppies - *opium poppies!*

Unfortunately, when they got to Chengtu, there was no longer a place for them at the Boarding School. The building had been burned ... after being hit by a bomb, probably. Millie and August were sent to the home of an older American Baptist couple that had no children of their own. Cousin, Vay Lovegren, says that Millie talked about holding tightly to the door knob and begging Papa not to leave her there, but he did. The couple was fairly strict. Millie cried not only when she was punished, but even more when little August was. It was not a happy time for them.

Next they went to live with a Canadian family who had five children of their own. It was traumatic for Millie. She said whenever August cried, she put her arm around him and said, "August, you mustn't cry, no matter how terrible it is." August recalls:

"Later Mildred and I stayed in different homes that had children our ages. I guess Papa and Mother paid folks for keeping us as we often stayed with families of other missions. I was in the home of a Dr. and Mrs. Stubbs who had a son my age. One morning we got word that Dr. Stubbs, who taught at the University of Chengtu, had been stabbed by an angry student. He died later that day, and I was immediately transferred to another home. Mrs. Stubbs and her son, John, returned to England shortly after this. I remember missing playing with John Stubbs. I have not heard anything about the Stubbs' since then.

"Mildred stayed some of the time in the home of the Moncrief family. They were Canadian missionaries and had girls Mildred's age. Another family I (August) stayed with was Dr. and Mrs. Willford, also of the Canadian Mission. He was a medical doctor and worked at the hospital on the university campus near their home. They had a son, also named John, who was one month older than I. We were best friends and also rivals in sports and academically. We were in the same grade. I remember that John was 'always' just a little bit better than I both in school and sports though I won often enough to help keep us friends. John and I used to sneak over to the hospital sometimes and look around, especially at the X-ray machine. Once John's father showed us the operating theatre and we were thrilled. I decided during those days that I wanted to be a doctor when I grew up. I remember those as pleasant days."

Mildred liked the fact that some of the children were American and some were Canadian, so the school celebrated holidays of both countries. One of her teachers dressed in quite modern clothes. She didn't even "look like a missionary". Mildred was also very pleased when her classmate, Jean Bridgeman, became a Christian; she seemed to feel a little part of her decision.

The school encouraged active participation in sports. Millie and August learned to play tennis and ride bicycles. Every year on Queen Victoria's birthday, there was an all day sports time of track and field events. Millie participated in throwing the shot put, running in the dashes, and doing the broad and high jumps. She also learned to fly the large, lovely Chinese butterfly kites.

One of the English ladies started a Girls' Guide Troop (like our Girl Scouts). Besides earning her badges, Millie learned some about nursing, nature, and camping with her troop. She enjoyed it.

Millie also had art and piano lessons at school. She learned a little about gardening. Each student had a small plot of land where a child could just dig, or they could plant vegetables or flowers or even trees.

The Canadian mission had plans to rebuild the boarding school on the University campus. This they did either in the fall of 1930 or the spring of 1931. August remembers,

"When the boarding school opened both Mildred and I were entered there. They had at least 20 students, as I recall, from kindergarten through the ninth grade. I remember that when I was ten, I graduated from the 7:00 PM bedtime to the 8:00 PM bedtime. I was so glad that I could stay up the extra hour. The odd thing is that I don't recall any difference in my sleeping habits caused by the change. When I went to bed, I went to sleep, and I woke up at the same time wide awake and ready to go."

Years later we visited the Boarding School

When little brother, Norman, arrived at the boarding school, he remembered many nights that were not so peaceful. Feuding war lords and their armies often fought battles on the hills right outside of Chengtu at night. Norman, trying to adjust to school so far from home, found it very hard to sleep when the noise of battle was so close and lasted so long into the night. Being a missionary child, separated from parents, and in an often hostile environment, is not always an easy way to grow up.

Mt. Omei

Way out in West China near Kiating where we lived was a beautiful, tall mountain called Mount Omei (now spelled Emei). Many people had summer homes part way up the slopes of this lovely mountain; in fact the President of China, Chiang Kai Shek had a vacation home there. American Baptist missionaries had a compound of bungalows for families to stay in while they escaped from the steamy summer heat. This was not only nice, but advisable for health reasons. The little houses were between the 5,000 and 6,000 foot altitude level which was cool enough, but not too far from the plains so that Papa could go down to Kiating by himself, a day's journey by foot.

Our family escaping the summer heat at Mt. Omei

So, sometime after school was out the family would journey to Mt. Omei. Coolies carried the luggage ... and sometimes us.

When we got tired, a Chinese coolie carried us piggyback for as long as we needed. Adults also could be carried if they got tired. The method for them was a sedan chair - two young men carried a person seated in a chair (with two long poles attached to it) on their shoulders - one man in front, the other behind. Millie later enjoyed this way of "mountain climbing".

Summer at Mt. Omei and later, Millie enjoying a sedan chair

Tennis was a game widely used for recreation in West China. Clay courts were not too expensive to build and maintain even on Mt. Omei where an area was leveled so that a court could be made. Papa was good at tennis and mother did fairly well, too. They used to play quite a bit on Mt. Omei in the summer. Millie and August got their own rackets when they were around ten years of age. They learned to play well not only at Mt. Omei, but also at home in Kiating, and at school in Chengtu. When missionaries were on furlough they bought rackets, extra strings, and balls packed in vacuum cans so there would be plenty of spares. Papa was good at restringing rackets when they needed it.

Several summers the family hiked to the peak of the mountain. From our bungalows, it was easily made in a day. At the top of the mountain was a fairly large Buddhist temple. There are actually many Buddhist temples on various levels along the stone trail. Faithful Buddhists believe they gain spiritual merit by climbing the mountain and worshipping in the temples.   In fact to a Buddhist, Mt. Omei is very special - one of the four "Holy Mountains" in all of China. The temples also are used for anyone who is climbing and needs rest, or is caught in a mountain storm. Usually there is some food as well as shelter in these temples.

At one of the temples, there was an interesting curiosity for Millie, August, and Norman.   One of the priests use to show people an artifact that he called "Buddha's tooth". It was about a foot tall by four inches, by three inches. It may have been some sort of petrified rock. Here is a picture of August and Norman on either side of the priest with the "tooth", while Millie is sitting on the temple steps watching.

The priest showing them Buddha's "tooth"

One of the very special things about the top of Mount Omei is the marvelous view of the Snowy Mountains, the Himalayas, the highest mountains in the world. So climbing this very special mountain are Buddhist pilgrims gaining merit, climbers who want to "conquer" the mountain, sightseers looking for a view of the

Snowy Ones, and lately, thrill-seeking, daring, young Chinese who hang glide off the sharp cliffs of the mountain to the rice paddies far, far, far below. I'm not sure the farmers in the plains appreciate this latest dangerous form of amusement.

Millie loved Mt. Omei. Even though the climb was strenuous, she always hoped to climb again to the top. In 1982, my brother Norman, his wife Viola, Millie and I (Edie) tried climbing it, but soon we were exhausted, so we contented ourselves with sitting near a cascading mountain stream by one of the temples, watching Millie talk to climbers. Many of these people were amazed at seeing Westerners there - much less one who spoke Mandarin with their own accent. They crowded around her listening to everything she had to say.

Millie attracted a crowd everywhere we went

Tourists on the trail at Mt. Omei

Edie, Norman, Viola and Millie resting by the trail

Eleven years later in 1993 when my niece went on a China tour with Millie, they also journeyed to Mt. Omei. Of course by this time Millie was older, 73 I believe. Also on this later tour was a former missionary to China, Astrid Peterson, who was in excellent health but *91* years young. My niece, Mimi Lanier, explains their trip this way...

"When we climbed Mt. Emei, Aunt Millie dutifully pointed us in the right direction, showing us the clearly marked and easily followed path up hundreds of stone stairs. I determined to climb the whole way up the gorgeous mountain and began plodding up the steps. It was quite a climb, and I was thankful that it wasn't very hot. I began to wonder how Aunt Millie and Astrid Peterson could make it up. Just a few minutes later, Aunt Millie came trotting by in her sedan chair, with two young Chinese men carrying her as nimbly as you please. She grinned her little grin and waved as they trotted past. And Astrid Peterson was in a chair right behind her.

(I didn't think there were sedan chairs anymore! - Edie)

"When I finally made it to the top huffing and puffing, Aunt Millie and Astrid were calmly waiting, gazing out into the clouds. It was very foggy at the top of the mountain with almost zero visibility. Aunt Millie was very disappointed to miss her Snowy Mountains. Just as we were leaving to begin our descent off the mountain, the clouds parted for just a minute, and we were able to see the beautiful Himalayas in the distance. I remarked to Aunt Millie, that I felt that that was God's special gift for her, and now looking back to her last trip to China, I'm sure it was."

"Delight thyself also in the Lord, and He will give thee the desires of thine heart" (Psalm 37:4).

Chapter Two

LIVING IN THE UNITED STATES

When our parents returned for furlough to the United States in 1932, we first visited relatives in Oregon and Washington. By this time, I was four years old and Millie was about thirteen. Our wonderful Aunt Cherry Langsea in Seattle had a very special gift for the four of us children - for seven years she had saved the Sunday comics to give to us. All the way to Minnesota in our Graham-Paige touring car, we read these funny papers, and we kept them for a while in Minneapolis - that was our library. It was not a time for giving expensive gifts. Many people were out of work. America was deep in the Great Depression.

Papa did some speaking but mainly during this furlough, Papa wanted to work on a Master's Degree at the University of Minnesota. However, it soon became apparent that the depression was so severe that we might not get to go back to China. Many people were out of work. Money was scarce for even the necessities of food and shelter. People could not be expected to give much to church and mission projects when they had so little themselves.

When mission boards looked for ways to cut expenses, one thing they began to note was the size of each missionary family. We were a family of six - four children! Obviously the cost for passage, as well as salary, and schooling was much higher for us than for the single missionaries or for a couple with no children. It seemed that we needed to be cut.

Although Papa was an engineer and had done building projects as well as evangelistic work on the foreign field, no such projects were now available. However, he had taught math classes

before going to China and was able to get a teaching job. We were
scraping along as many others were when a new disaster hit us.
Papa's health deteriorated and his strength dwindled. Papa had
bladder *cancer*. He had to have an operation. The doctors said
even if they were able to get the cancer out, they expected it to
return. As far as the doctors were concerned, Papa's chances of
survival were very slim. They removed the cancer, and Papa lived
to a ripe old age. Isn't it wonderful that God can heal, when doctors
have given up?

Making Do

God also provided for our basic needs by putting it on our
wonderful Uncle Samuel Nelson's heart to loan us money for
years. We weren't poor people - we just didn't have money, but
during the depression few people did. Everyone was learning to
"make do" (to stretch things as far as they could go). For instance,
Millie's high school wardrobe consisted of three blouses and two
skirts. Mother wore an ugly lime-green dress for her "Sunday
Best" for years. Yuck!

One little thing that was an unhappy surprise to Millie in
America was *who did the housework.* The answer seemed to be -
the mother and the oldest daughter. In China, the Chinese servants
did the housework, but no one seemed to have servants in
America. With our very limited funds, we couldn't have paid for
anyone to help if they had been available. Luckily, I was too
young to help.

As children, we learned to eat simple snacks. In the summer,
we had red rhubarb growing in the garden. There was sour clover
in the grass, and elm seeds everywhere. As young as I was, even I
learned to slip the outside skins so I could eat the tiny kernels.

Christmas time was exciting fun. Every year we got several
presents: a comb, bobby-pins, a new toothbrush (if we needed it)
and a new pair of socks. All were nicely wrapped in the Sunday
newspaper funnies. In our stockings, we usually got four or five

pieces of hard candy, some nuts, an apple or an orange, and usually another little present. We felt that we did well. Can you imagine any child being satisfied with such gifts nowadays?

One day, someone gave our family a little pad of different colored papers. Millie and brother August thought of a wonderfully ingenious way of using them. With the different colors, they began to make play money like the money in a friend's Monopoly set, a favorite but expensive game. They found a large piece of cardboard and painstakingly drew their own board. It took a long time, but they drew it well. I thought the "go to jail" policeman was a perfect copy. The little trains were well done, too. I believe rocks were the first moving "men" before they used buttons. Even the property ownership papers, Chance, and Community Chest were drawn correctly.

I'm not sure if this hand-drawn set infringed on any copyright laws, but it was more treasured, and better taken care of than any store-bought game. They played with it for years. Other children thought it was more fun to play with the handmade set than the real ones. I wasn't allowed to play, because I was still considered to be too young.

There is a certain amount of skill, pride, imagination, and self reliance that comes from "making do" with the materials on hand. Millie would be called on to "make do" many times on the mission field. Let me mention one example:

During her first term in Guilin, Millie especially thanked me for sending her a Bible story coloring book. It was a silly, joke Christmas present. However, after the Communists took over their city and they could no longer import Christian materials, Millie traced pages from the coloring book for children to color in Sunday School. She also traced figures to make her own Bible flannelgraph stories. When she was forced to leave Guilin, she left the coloring book behind, so the Chinese Christians could continue to use it.

Again I'm not sure about copyright infractions, but, "Thank you" to whoever drew that simple Bible story coloring book. It was well used for God's work in China.

First Swedish Baptist Church

The house that Papa rented for us in Minneapolis was within walking distance of schools and the University of Minnesota; however, there was not a "proper" church close by. Although our parents were officially American Baptist Missionaries, they were always members of a Swedish Baptist Church. You see, Swedish Baptists, German Baptists, Russian Baptists, and other ethnic groups had no mission-sending agencies of their own, so they sent their missionaries with full support under the American Baptist Foreign Mission Societies. So, my brother August tells me, every Sunday we Swedes drove quite a ways to attend the First Swedish Baptist Church of Minneapolis. Our folks knew and spoke Swedish, but we kids only spoke English and Mandarin Chinese. On alternate Sundays, the church service was in Swedish or English. Luckily, Sunday School for the children was always in English. On the Swedish-speaking Sundays, the children played in the Sunday School rooms or outside during church.

Millie was so very young when she accepted Jesus as her Savior, that she did not remember it, but she knew Jesus was in her heart as far back as she could recall. She was baptized during the fall of 1933 by the Swedish pastor, Rev. Anton Sjolund. All of us children accepted Jesus as our Savior very early, and only August remembers the experience. Even without a specific memory of giving our lives to the Lord, however, Millie, Norman and I were convinced through the years that our commitment to the Lord and His presence in our lives is very real.

Our family liked to sing. Papa and Mother joined the choir almost right away, and soon Millie and August were singing in the choir, too. Millie and Mother sang soprano - even singing solos in church. Papa sang bass and August could handle either bass or tenor. I guess brother, Norman, had to sit with me.

A few years later our church had services every Sunday morning in English. Some adult Sunday School classes were in Swedish, and there was a Sunday afternoon Swedish service. By 1940, few of the young adults knew or understood Swedish anymore. In order to reach more people, the church changed its name to Bethlehem Baptist Church. It is still near downtown Minneapolis, and has a very active body of believers.

The church had a wonderful group of young people that did many activities together. Millie and August were very active in the church "gang". When we were all quarantined because Millie had scarlet fever, the gang sent her a pot of tulips that she thought was very special and expensive. She was probably right! In those days, only rich people sent flowers. This group provided both Millie and August with some life-long friends.

One thing Millie loved to do was go with the church young people to conferences at Medicine Lake and Mound. They made her feel spiritually charged up and refreshed. The family went to Medicine Lake, too, since it was nearby in East St. Paul. This large park with its many Indian mounds is made special by Battle Creek River which runs through it. I liked swimming in Medicine Lake as much as Millie did until my head went underwater when I stepped in a hole. I came up coughing and convinced that I nearly drowned. I was afraid to go swimming again for two years!

Millie also loved Bible camps. For two years, she was a camp counselor at Camp Bethel at beautiful Lake Minnetonka which is situated just west of Minneapolis surrounded by beautiful forest. She loved the large, blue lakes of that area. Many of the city dwellers had homes along the shores and there were many picnic and recreation areas nearby.

Millie was also active in the YWCA Girl Reserves throughout her high school years. She spent one summer as a lifeguard and counselor at a Y camp in Minnesota. Because she herself got so much blessing from these camps and conferences, Millie wanted others to share these experiences. Camping and youth retreats later became an important part of her missionary work with young people.

That Wonderful Class of 1937

Most of us go through high school making a few lasting friends and barely knowing the others in our class. We rarely see our classmates after we graduate. Millie's class at Marshall High School was different. Right to begin with, they adopted her. She was thirteen when she came to America and entered the ninth grade. They found her interesting. She was from foreign places. She had been in a good Canadian school in China and knew English with a Canadian accent and expressions, like "jolly well" and "my stars" - decidedly *not* American. Some of her studies, especially history, had been taught from a different viewpoint. Remember, Canada fought on the other side against those independence-seeking states in both the Revolutionary War and the War of 1812. Millie was good in geography. She knew quite a bit about China, and she could name all the Canadian Provinces and their capitals. She didn't know very much about that country south of Canada that was now her home.

Her teacher asked her to talk about China and show some things from her birthplace. Mother helped her prepare a little suitcase with some Chinese artifacts. She didn't remember ever talking in front of anybody before, and she felt scared to death as she stood behind her desk with her knees knocking. The first thing she said out loud was, "Oh, I'm so nervous." The class answered, "Don't be nervous; it's just us." Since they seemed so friendly and laid back, she was soon able to relax and just talk to them. They became her good friends all the way through high school and kept up with her through the years.

The school sponsored roller skating parties for high school and college students at the Minneapolis Arena. August tells me that he, Norman and Millie enjoyed the Roller Derby Nights, although Millie never felt she was a good skater. She enjoyed going to the football and basketball games, and to the school senior class plays.

She joined the debate team, the English Honorary Club, and she received a Recognition Certificate for outstanding service rendered to the school during the year, 1936-1937.

There were two people in the class that took "keeping in touch" with their high school friends as a lifetime hobby. They wrote the news of various class members, and when there was a difficulty or a problem, they would write to encourage classmates to pray for them and to send cards. This was even more amazing since Marshall was a public high school! Every five years, the class has met together, arranging the time so that Millie would be on furlough and could come. In 1992, they had the 55th anniversary of their graduation from high school.

Some of Millie's classmates and their spouses went to China with her on tours. Millie was very thankful for her Marshall High School class and for their support and encouragement through the years.

The Laundry

After Millie graduated from Marshall High School she attended the University of Minnesota in Minneapolis within walking distance from home. She felt lost and unhappy among so many students. The next year she decided to attend the much smaller Swedish school, Bethel Junior College in Saint Paul, Minnesota. Here she was much happier and she made much better grades. She was also able to participate in fun things like girls basketball, girls chorus, and mission teams. She enjoyed that year to the fullest.

In 1939, Millie graduated from Bethel Junior College with an Associate of Arts degree. In those days, that was often all that was needed to be a teacher. Men who were going to be pastors went from the college to the other school on campus, Bethel Seminary. Two years of college and three years of seminary was the proper period of training for a pastor or an evangelistic missionary.

The summer that Millie finished her two years of college, the family again moved to a completely different area - Birmingham,

Alabama - where Papa had a job teaching at Howard College. Millie wanted to continue her education, but there was not enough money for two children, and brother August now needed his chance. As long as Millie had to work anyway, she decided she would rather stay North with her friends and maybe get a year or two at the seminary. It was much cheaper than Howard College.

So, in the fall of 1939, Millie was still in St. Paul going to Bethel Seminary. How did she pay her way? She and another girl started a laundry! I'm not sure what she knew about men's shirts, but she must have learned. Students dressed more formally then, and this was especially true of young men who were studying to be pastors. White shirts, ties, slacks, and coats were the proper seminary attire. Of course, since there was no such thing as perma-press, all shirts had to be washed, dampened and ironed. Fellows tried to be careful so that they could wear a shirt at least two days, but even so, they needed three clean ones every week. Millie and her friend did all right.

One Easter time, a young man brought in a really nice suit that he had been given. He wanted to wear it on Easter Sunday morning when he was going to preach, but the suit was too big. He didn't have the money to take it to a tailor. He asked Millie if she could make the suit smaller so he could wear it. She sat up most of the night remodeling that suit, and later she wondered how she had the courage. I guess when one is twenty, one will try amazing things.

Not only did Millie make ends meet that school year in the laundry, but she learned a lot. Even though she was a girl, she was allowed to take the regular theology courses - Greek and all. She also had another great job - reading to a blind seminary student. His main textbook was *Strong's Theology*. She could hardly pronounce the words, much less understand them. She read it, the blind man interpreted it to her, and they both learned.

Our family after we moved to Birmingham

To Swim or Not to Swim

Mother knew how to swim. I guess that is what you would call it. She could propel herself in water for short distances with a motion that I can best describe as a side-stroke flop. It kept most of her face above water and it kept her from drowning, but that was the best you could say for it.

Papa was strong and swam well, with good strokes, and was especially impressive doing a fast Australian crawl. He enjoyed being in water. Mother did not, but it was she who was insistent that all her children learn to swim, not only for safety, but she considered it the perfect exercise.

In Minneapolis where we lived in the thirties, there were very few swimming pools but, after all, Minnesota is the land of 10,000 lakes which range from ponds to the mighty Lake Superior. On occasion, we went to a lake and tried swimming. Millie became very good at it. She even took training to become a Senior Life Guard. Impressive? It was in those days.

When Millie joined us in Birmingham a year later, she had to find a job, not only for expenses but also for college books and tuition for her last year in college. Jobs were still scarce. She was so *blessed.* She found a nice job that summer, not too far from home, as a lifeguard at the big Cascade Plunge pool.

This is part of Camp Mary Munger where Millie was lifeguard

It wasn't long before we realized that something was not right. Fellow Baptist Christians were shocked by Millie. She had a job at a public pool! She wore a bathing suit! We didn't understand what the problem was. A term was used that we had never heard before - *mixed bathing*. What? Evidently, good Baptist boys and girls in the South did not swim together. At their Baptist summer camps children were encouraged to swim, but only because the camps were just for boys, or just for girls. Bathing suits were never considered proper attire in mixed company.

The South was almost as strange a culture change for us as when we came from China to Minnesota. So many Baptist men smoked, often just outside the church door ... including some pastors! The Christians allowed their young people to go to movies, and even to go to dances! We had never considered doing such evil things. Yet here, we were being the apparent sinful ones.

When we realized the situation, (surprisingly) Mother did not encourage Millie to quit her job. I think she thought such Southern ideas were silly. Millie was really lucky to have a good job.

However, in a little while, God intervened. Millie saw a boy in distress, floundering near the edge of the pool. Instead of diving in, or climbing down from her lifeguard chair she jumped down onto the cement and broke her foot. The ungrateful, "drowning" boy was suddenly able to swim to the edge under his own power.

Obviously a person with a large cast on their leg does not make a good lifeguard! The job was gone. The next two summers Millie was again hired as a lifeguard, but this time at a proper girls camp.

"Then let us no more pass judgment on one another, but rather decide never to put a stumbling block, or hindrance in the way of a brother. I know and am persuaded in the Lord Jesus that nothing is unclean in itself; but it is unclean for anyone who thinks it unclean" (Romans 14:13-14).

Preparing to Go

Millie loved to travel. She used to say that she needed to marry a millionaire ... or a missionary ... so that she could see the world. Well, she never married at all. By the time she graduated from college after taking her last year at Howard in Birmingham, her commitment to the Lord and to missions was so strong that she never considered seriously dating anyone who wasn't planning to go to the mission field. To further prepare herself for that calling she attended and graduated from Southwestern Seminary in Fort Worth, Texas.

1943-44 found two members of our family in uniform

By 1944, Millie was prepared to be a missionary in China. She applied to the Southern Baptists who were willing to send her as soon as she passed their exams - the first was on theological questions and her statement of her faith in Jesus as Savior; the second was a complete medical exam; the third was a psychological exam to see if she could stand against the possible rigors of life as a single missionary. Millie was the most concerned about the third. How do you act? What do you say?

She went to the psychiatrist's office and was glad to talk to another lady who was waiting. She explained to the lady how nervous she was. They talked and joked together. Millie was a little more relaxed when she was finally called into the doctor's office. She answered his questions very cautiously and hopefully correctly. When the interview was over, she told him she was thankful because she was worried about making a good impression and hoped he would "pass" her. He explained that he was one of two interviewers that she would have, and after that the two doctors would consult together and make their report, but he felt the report would be favorable. Oh dear! Another one!

On her way out she asked the receptionist when her other appointment would be. She was informed that she had already talked to the first doctor here in the outer office. The first psychiatrist had already filled out her report. Oh my! What in the world had she said to that nice, friendly, joking lady? Somehow they both passed her.

She was appointed, she was ready, there was plenty of money for her salary and passage, *but* there was *no place to go!* The whole world was at war. To help her brush up on her Mandarin skills, she was sent to language school in Berkeley, California.

That was nice because we had several relatives in California. One family lived very near the main railroad track she would travel going to the Bay Area. Millie hoped she would be able to see their house as she neared the small farm outside of Turlock. Suddenly she was surprised to see not only the house, but Aunt Edna, and cousin, June Bruce, waving hands and dish towels at the train as it passed. She felt this was rather unusual, but very friendly. When she was visiting later, she asked if they waved that enthusiastically at every train that passed. No, of course not! They explained that the Lindbergs were on that train and promised to wave at them if they were outside when the train came by. They had seen them on the train and waved.

The Bruce's were very welcome relatives. Millie was glad she was with them when she unexpectedly lost a pesky appendix. They cared for her until she was well again.

At the language school in Berkeley, Millie met Fay Taylor. Fay used to read to her or tell her stories as they ironed or did other housework. One time Millie said, "Fay, don't tell me all of your stories now. We might have to live on the same mission station for the next forty years." Unfortunately for both, this didn't happen, but in the next fifty years they were to travel, play, study, and share together whenever they met in cities in America and all over the Far East.

Millie quickly became proficient in her native Mandarin under the tutelage of her excellent language teachers. She went to the local Chinese Baptist Church in happy anticipation and got a terrible shock. They didn't speak *her* Chinese. They talked that "unmelodious, guttural, wordy" Cantonese. The two Chinese languages were not at all the same, like the difference between French and German. Millie was thankful that she spoke Mandarin and vowed then and there that she would never learn Cantonese.

Six years later, she was living in Hong Kong and Macau where Cantonese was the Chinese language that was known and spoken. In spite of her vow, it was with great effort that she had to learn it. She wasn't as prepared as she thought. Later it was a great blessing for her to know both Mandarin and Cantonese.

"For My thoughts are not your thoughts, neither are your ways My ways, says the Lord. For as the heavens are higher than the earth, so are My ways higher than your ways and My thoughts than your thoughts" (Isaiah 55:8-9).

Chapter Three

THE GUILIN YEARS

Going Home to China

At last World War II was over. By late 1946, returning missionaries and new missionaries were able to go overseas to their mission fields. Millie not only got to go on a ship full of these missionaries, but also had the blessing of having our parents returning to China on the same steamer. This is how Millie described her journey in a letter to Aunt Anna and Uncle Will Lempke:

April 1, 1947

Dear Aunt Anna and Uncle Will,

The trip took longer than I had anticipated, but the Orient always has moved more slowly than our America. Our ship, the SS Marine Lynx, sailed out under the Golden Gate Bridge on December 15, 1946, just at sunset - one of the most beautiful and unusual that I have seen. It seemed to be a blessing from God on our journey.

The sea was unusually rough in the crossing. Accommodations were very crowded and not too adequate, especially for the mothers with small children, but the company was wonderful. To travel together with more than 400 other missionaries is a privilege one has perhaps only once in a lifetime, if then. My own parents were in this group of old and new friends. The opportunities of listening to the wisdom and spiritual experiences of older missionaries in the afternoon conferences and the evening services will always be an inspiring memory to me.

The waves quieted, and the sun shone as we neared Shanghai. In a strange way, I felt at home again. We reached Shanghai on New Year's Eve. We were greeted joyfully by missionaries and Chinese Christians alike. It made me feel very happy and yet very unworthy, too, to see how eagerly the ones over here were waiting for us. My parents debarked in Shanghai, bound for West China, while I stayed on the ship with the others going to South China.

Two days later, we saw the awe inspiring rocks that bank Hong Kong Harbor. It is beautiful, yet ruins from the war can be seen in many places, and several great ghost ships can be seen sticking their prows or hulks up through the blue water.

A river steamer carried us from Hong Kong to Canton. We had some stormy weather, but at each new port or city, the sun shone for us. Even the weather seemed to welcome us to our new home. During our two week stay in Canton, I was able to meet several missionary friends who had also recently come from America. We were privileged to attend the first graduation exercises from the Poi In Bible School since 1941, and also the first capping of nurses since the beginning of the Japanese invasion of World War II.

During this time, I received my first real picture of China's terrible need, as in a block just outside the Baptist Compound one evening, I saw two blind beggars lying prone on the street, desperately thin, and very scantily dressed. They were moaning out to passers-by for help. I was cold in my sweater and heavy coat. They are a symbol to me of all the sorrow that is China today. Sometimes sadness is mixed with a little bit of comedy, as was the case yesterday when an elderly gentleman came up to me while I was in a shop, and held out his hand. I was rather puzzled but decided the old fellow was trying to be friendly, so I shook hands with him in as genteel way as I could. He looked surprised. Later Missionary Lawton who had seen this said with a dry smile, "That is certainly an original way of confronting a beggar."

Mr. Lawton left by train for Kweilin shortly after our arrival in Canton. He took practically all our baggage. We were to follow a week later on a plane but because of bad weather, it was over two weeks before the plane was able to come in. It was two and a half more days before our plane actually took aff again. Air travel in China is very uncertain as yet, and also rather dangerous. It was pouring rain when we took off. We flew through a snowstorm, but the sun was shining when we landed safely on the part of the airport runway that wasn't broken up by bomb craters. We thanked God for the good safe trip. I thank you for your prayers for me as I traveled along. The Lord brought us through that day and all the other days.

A few days later, we were saddened by the news of two plane crashes. On the plane that crashed near Hankow, every missionary and child had been with us on the Marine Lynx ship. We knew them. Only the Vick baby lived, although the father lived long enough to dictate a letter as to what should be done with the baby. Why should it have happened? All we know is the Lord called them all to come up higher, while he stirs the rest of us left here to work more earnestly for His Kingdom's cause.

The actual sight of Kweilin was a shock to me. It had been hard hit during the war. I had never seen such mass destruction of a whole city, or people so desperately poverty stricken. Ninety per cent of Kweilin was completely demolished either by air raids or by the scorched earth policy. The Baptist compound itself looks like a graveyard of old Roman buildings.

Yet the spirit of the people is amazing. There are few beggars in the city. Everywhere buildings are going up. Many are being built of split bamboo and mud plaster with a little stolen brick for the foundation, but they are still going up.

Coolie woman re-building Guilin

Hope has come again into the people's hearts, and with that hope has come a marvelous interest in and yearning to know the truths of Christianity, and what it can mean to them. The National University and Middle Schools located here, which before were alien to Christianity, now open their doors eagerly to it. In the evening services, all kinds of people - from school principals, teachers, students, bankers, government officials to the lowly coolie women who wear rags and cannot even afford to buy a needle to mend their clothes - come forward with equal eagerness to inquire into the Gospel of Christ. How thrilling! Pray for us as we seek to help here.

Lovingly, Your grandniece, Mildred

Getting Started

Because Millie already spoke Mandarin Chinese and had recently studied it in San Francisco, she did not need the extensive language study normally required of a new missionary. By January, 1947, she was in Guilin, a beautiful green place of strange rounded mountain/hills, a pretty river, and interesting deep caves.

Today Guilin is one of the main foreign tourist cities because of its unusually lovely scenery. The poet, Han Yu, of the Tang Dynasty wrote of Guilin, "The river forms a green gauze belt, the mountains are like jade hairpins." Many tourists have wondered if there could be a more peaceful place on earth.

Guilin - "the most peaceful place on earth"

There the fishermen take advantage of the large cormorant population to aid them in fishing by tieing a string around their long necks. Then, when they catch a fish, expecting to have a fine meal, the fisherman pulls the bird in and retrieves the fish for himself. Once in a while, the cormorant is allowed to swallow his fish so he won't become discouraged.The name has always been pronounced the same, however the city has been spelled in English with a K-Kweilin, or a Q-Queilin, or with the current G-Guilin.

On Millie's second day in Guilin, two students came from the University to talk to one of the senior missionaries to ask if he would come to their campus and speak to their Christian Fellowship. He said to them, "We have a young lady here now. Why don't you ask her?" Millie was twenty-six. He introduced her to the two young people, a fellow and a girl, who spoke to her in English. They asked if she could ride a bicycle. Millie answered that she thought so, though she hadn't ridden one recently.

By Sunday, they had provided her with a bicycle to ride out to the campus which was located on the edge of the city. She was very pleased that the students spoke standard Northern Mandarin to each other - the language and dialect that she could understand. They asked her to come back again, so Millie started going regularly to the campus, visiting the girls in their dorms and joining them in various other extra-curricular activities such as parties and picnics, athletic events and even the Chinese opera.

She enjoyed these students very much and realized she was better qualified to work with them than to counsel women and children which was her original assignment. After all, she had already worked with young people as a counselor, lifeguard, and crafts instructor for several summers.

One of the missionaries in Shanghai said to her one day, "Let me tell you something about student work in China: You follow your students. After they graduate, you still keep in touch."

Millie asked, "How can you do that? They are graduating every year! They would get to be so many!"

"The Lord will show you which ones are your responsibility," she answered. "You can't teach them what they need to know in just two or three years about living this Christian life. It's a long haul."

Millie could see the truth in what she said, so she decided, "Well, all right, I'll try!"

At the time of her death Millie, was still in touch with three of her students she met her very first year in Guilin. All three got out to Hong Kong, and eventually moved to North America. They are grandparents now, who have lived wonderful lives, and through the years have been special, really rewarding friends, old buddies - Phoebe Cheung of Miami, Florida, Victor Leung of Richmond, British Columbia, Canada, and C.T. Wong of Vancouver, British Columbia, Canada.

Friends in Guilin - Phoebe, Ling Yuen, Kin and others

Maryknoll Mission Friends

When Millie came to Guilin, the Catholic Maryknoll Mission had a strong group of priests and nuns there. The city was in ruins and surviving was the first order of the day. The Catholics cooperated readily with the Southern Baptist Mission and with other Christian groups. During the long years of Japanese occupation during World War II, cooperation was their means of survival. A southern Baptist missionary, Dr. Bill Wallace, had remained in China during the war, hiding his hospital in caves, so that he could continue to minister to the Chinese people. No one reported him to the Japanese occupation army since they were dependent on each other for their survival. They were united against a common enemy.

Millie got acquainted with some of the priests in this way: Millie planned a short vacation - a bus trip to the South. The Baptist Mission leaders did not feel that it was wise for her to go by bus, although she had done it before, so they arranged for her to travel with three priests. The Fathers, who had been left with a lot of World War II equipment, were delivering a truck to Dr. Wallace in Wuchow. It was cheaper for the United States government to leave large items behind, than pay for them to be shipped back to America. The generous Catholics were sharing their "booty" with other missionaries and Christians.

Millie and the three Catholic Fathers rode together in the truck, one priest driving and two in the back flatbed. Millie always got to be in the passenger seat. This way she got to talk to each priest personally while he was driving. At night they stopped at Catholic church compounds and Millie slept in the convents with the nuns.

Millie especially liked Father Glass. He called that particular expedition, "Goldilocks and the Three Bears". One day Father Glass said, "Millie, you preach the gospel, and win as many as you can to the Lord, and I'll preach the gospel, and win as many as I

can to the Lord, and maybe we can get this province Christian."
Some of the Maryknoll Missionaries were quite evangelistic
Christians.

All three of the priests smoked. Of course, this was before
anyone realized how harmful smoking could be. As Millie was
having breakfast with her priests and two other local smoking
priests, she asked, "Is it necessary when you take your vows as a
Catholic priest to say that you smoke?"

They laughed. One of them said, "Oh yes, when I took my
vows and they asked me if I smoked, I said, 'Of course.'"

Father Glass replied, "Really, we don't all smoke."

Millie retorted, "I surely haven't seen one that doesn't,
everyone here seems to smoke."

Father Glass said, "Let me tell you a story: There was a new
priest who came to Guilin. Almost immediately he was invited to
a meal at the home of one of the local believers, and he accepted
gladly. Before the meal was served, the host offered the new priest
some cigarettes, but the priest said, 'No thank you, I don't smoke.'
Although the host was a bit surprised, he didn't say anything. As
they sat down at the table each place had a wine glass and a tea cup
among other things. Before they ate the host offered a toast to his
guests. The priest picked up his tea cup for the toasting. The host
thought this priest was really inexperienced and didn't understand.
He explained that toasting was done, not with a tea cup but with the
little wine glass. The priest answered 'Thank you very much, but I
don't drink, so I will toast with my tea cup.' Now the host was
very surprised. 'You don't smoke and you don't drink?' he asked.
'Show me your papers! I don't believe you are a Catholic priest.'"

The fathers all laughed; they thought it was a good joke.
Millie was glad they could joke with her, and that they treated her
as a friend.

Despite natural differences in theology and practice, the
Catholics proved to be good friends. Even when Millie and the

others had to leave Guilin at the Communist takeover in the early 1950's, the Maryknoll Sisters brought apples to the train, so they would have something to eat on the way to Canton. Millie didn't know where they could have found such a delicious gift.

Years later, one of the Guilin nuns became Mother Superior at a convent in Hong Kong, and she and Millie met not only there, but were together in a special meeting in Kobe, Japan.

When Millie returned to Guilin almost thirty years later, she was surprised that the Catholic Christians still welcomed the Baptist missionaries as if they were their own. Millie remembered one lady who burst through a crowd and greeted her with great joy. She told Millie that she had been helped tremendously at the Baptist Hospital and she was very grateful, so much so that she asked for Millie's address in Hong Kong, and wrote to her several times, thanking her again.

Millie brought Bibles into Guilin to give to her Baptist friends, but there were not enough to go around. Later that fall when journeyman Shelby White took a tour into China that included Guilin, Millie gave him Bibles to take to a Chinese friend she called "Big Brother." He couldn't find the friend. However, a fellow tour member knew some of the Maryknoll Christians who were glad to help Shelby. They personally took him to the Baptist Christians where he met "Big Brother" and delivered the Bibles.

"Holy Father, keep them in Thy name, which Thou hast given me, that they may be one, even as we are one" (John 17:11b).

A Trip By Sampan

If there was a need, Millie had the will, and she would find a way. Missionary Fay Taylor told about being asked (along with other women missionaries) to lead a Bible School and a Conference in Wuchow. This is how she described the travel arrangements:

The most adventurous trip I took with Millie was down the West River in China from Guilin to Wuchow. Millie chartered a 25-foot sampan for five of us lady missionaries. The crew consisted of a lady skipper, her old mother, her young daughter, and three oarsmen. Oh yes, there was also a small, black and white piglet aboard. The four-and-a-half day trip was exciting, potentially dangerous, and it was an incredible journey.

We had to lay over several hours in a small village because of rising flood waters. We had to pass over frightening rapids, and then tie up at night with hundreds of other small craft because of the robbers that used the waterway. In typical Millie style, while the boat was tied up in one place, she led us to visit some missionaries in that small village that she had met somewhere, someplace. We had tea, and we had refreshing showers. Before returning to our little sampan, we bought some vegetables. We continued on our way when the water had receded a few feet.

We reached Wuchow safely in a tremendous rainstorm, but we were safe, and able to help in the Bible School and the Conference. Another wonderful experience was that there we met the famed doctor, 'Bill Wallace of China'.

"Millie, Millie, I would have missed so much had I not met you!"

Witnessing While There Is Yet Time

The political situation in China was very threatening. Before the Chinese government could recover from the wreckage and ravages of World War II, there was a recurring insurgence of their old, violent enemy - The Red Bandits! The weakened government forces could not withstand the new wave of Communist ideology. General Mao and his bandit forces took over China, province by province. Persecution was violent and came in every form against body, mind and soul - complete with physical torture and brainwashing.   Time was again running out for the China missionaries.

Dr. Wallace was imprisoned, tortured and beaten to death although the government issued a report that he had hung himself. Other prisoners were able to report the truth, however. He had no evidence of hanging. Instead, his body was black and blue and swollen throughout from the terrible beatings he suffered. Fellow prisoners had observed the torture he endured before his death. Other Chinese simply disappeared without cause, without explanation.

Here is a letter Millie wrote at that tense time to seminary friends, Sara Ruth and Charles Mullins, who had other friends in Shanghai who had already gone through "the liberation" of the Communists.   Southern Baptists were having urgent prayer meetings for their China missionaries. Millie wrote:

Baptist Mission

Kweilin, Kwangsi, China

April 10, 1949

Dear Sara Ruth and Charles,

We thank and praise the Lord for the peace and relative quiet He continues still to bless us with in Guilin.   In many parts of China the 'red bear' pants hotly behind the 'bamboo curtain', but hearts here are relatively unaroused.   Prices are high, refugees many, but businesses go on as before. Why do we have this peace? The only reason that we can give is that the Lord must still have 'much people in this city' that must be won and taught to follow Him. Many are young people - students. I want to tell you about them.

When I first came to China I thought that, like my mother, I would work with women and children. But in Kweilin, I found the women spoke the colloquial language almost entirely.   At first, they had great difficulty understanding me, and I had greater difficulty understanding them, but the young people in their high schools and colleges were studying pure Mandarin and English. This language contact, plus the fact that I was young, too, gave me a wedge with these young folk from the start.

China's youth today live much closer to the spiritual world for good or for evil than we were conscious of in America. The darkness and sin in the minds and lives of young people growing up in the cities and villages where there is absolutely no Christian influence of any kind, where the Bible has never been heard of, can scarcely be imagined by Americans who breathe the influence of a Christian heritage. Yet these youths have a terrible hunger for truth and for a way of life that would lift them and their country out of despair. They turn to us not by just ones or twos, but by the dozens.

To our new student center have come young people from practically every school in the city (the ten high schools, the colleges, the medical school and the nurses training center). They ask, "What is truth?" "Are all men sinners?" "What is sin anyway?" "Is there a God?" "What does the cross mean?" "How can I learn to pray?" "Why are there so many kinds of churches?" The responsibility of leading them aright is great. Just plain conversation is much simpler than the words one needs in speaking about one's soul's destiny. We do not fear, because the Holy Spirit can be our interpreter.

Nearly a hundred students attended the Spring Conference, eighty of them living with us on our mission compound for three-and-a-half days. Fifteen girls stayed in our home and *sixty-five* boys stayed with Oz Quick. Yes, we wondered where he put them, too! Each morning they looked like they had slept passably well. We all met together for meals in the large basement. It is the first time I tried peanuts on my breakfast cereal - really quite good, you know. Our speakers were very inspirational and many youths came forward for prayer during the decision time. The conference theme song,

"I'd Rather Have Jesus," seemed even more beautiful in Chinese.

We have praised God in these weeks since the retreat not only for the wonderful memory of the conference, but also for the continuing work God is doing. There have been decisions to follow Christ on the various campuses as there were at the conference, and the end is not yet.

One of our students' important questions is the problem of finding a Christian mate. In China, this question has a few wrinkles added. Even in modern China, parents have a strong voice in who their son or daughter marries. Himmy and Juanita, two fine Christians, have been separated by Juanita's parents for several months because they want her to marry a man with more wealth and position. Even though her parents are active Christians in our Canton church, they are behaving toward their daughter like the heathen ways of Old China. This is common even today. There is a second problem. So few girls even have a high school education in comparison to the many men in higher education. There are fifteen men to each girl at Kwangsi National University. Our Christian men don't want to marry the uneducated, heathen girls that their parents have picked out for them, but who can they substitute? We must win more girls to Christ. Pray for me to do my part in this matter.

Thank you for your thoughts and prayers for me in these past months. I pray for you and your work too.

Loving wishes always,

Millie Lovegren

P.S. Conditions in China are daily getting more tense. The Communists crossed the river day before yesterday. Keep praying for God's will to be done in this tragic land. Only He can help!

Huanyao

When Millie was a young new missionary working with students in Guilin, she would often go with them to special events. One of these events was a concert and a Chinese opera held at the far university, 18 miles from town. At the program, she soon noticed a young man who was playing a Chinese violin. He seemed very happy; in fact, vivacious. His eyes sparkled as he played the instrument easily. She had a strong impression as she watched him: *Pray for that man.* She thought it was strange to feel so strongly about him since he was just part of the orchestra, but she started praying for him.

When they left the concert to return to the city, he happened to be on the same crowded bus. Millie smiled at him across the bus, and their eyes caught. She remarked, "You play very well; I enjoyed it." He thanked her, and then started to sing in English, *Carry Me Back to Old Virginny.*

Millie was quite amused and touched. Since the crowd was so thick, she didn't get to really talk to him and he got off near the campus.

Later when Millie described him, asking some fellow students who that violin player was, they didn't seem to know his name. One even questioned, "Millie, why are you asking about him? He's not a Christian. He is not interested."

Millie continued to feel a burden for him and she prayed for him. A few times, she would see him at a distance as they were both going places on their bicycles. Early one Sunday morning as she was riding her bike to the University Christian Fellowship, he was coming from the campus. She decided she was going to find out his name. As she stopped her bike, she said, "Hello; good morning! What is your name?"

He answered. "I'm sorry, I don't have time to go to the Christian Fellowship this morning."

What a strange reply. She didn't know what to say after that. Then he laughed and said, "Oh, you asked my name, didn't you?"

"Yes, I did ask your name, but since you brought it up, why don't you come to Christian Fellowship next Sunday morning?"

"I will," he replied, "And my name is Yu Huanyao."

The next Sunday he was there, and Huanyao continued to come to the Christian Fellowship for several weeks. It was a time of real confusion. The Communist bandits were conquering the central part of China and coming closer to Guilin every day. Quite a few of the university professors left the campus, and were trying to leave China. They hoped to get to Hong Kong, Taiwan, or even overseas. Students were leaving, too. One Sunday, Huanyao wasn't there so Millie asked about him. Someone had heard that he received word that his mother was very ill and he should try to come home. It was not going to be an easy trip. To get to Hunan, his home province, he had to get through the front lines of fighting between the Nationalists and the Communists.

Usually after the University Fellowship meeting Millie bicycled to the Baptist Church for Sunday School and Worship Service but that morning, she went home to pray for Huanyao. She was led to pray, "If it is Your will, Lord, do something (not hurt it, but something), so that the plane won't arrive today." She really felt that Christians needed to talk and pray with him before he left. In those uncertain times, no one knew what would happen or if he would ever get back to Guilin. Millie was especially concerned for Huanyao because even though he was coming to the Christian meetings, he had not made any profession of faith in Jesus Christ as Savior.

Millie did get to part of the morning service at church, then when it was over, she went to the airline offices where she asked about the plane.

"It was very strange," they said, "but the plane did not arrive today; something delayed it. It will be here tomorrow."

Millie thanked the Lord and went to the University to find Huanyao. He had not come back. One of the students knew about a relative of his in Guilin. Millie found him there, and told him she would like him to come to the mission house the next day before he went to the airport.

Sure enough, the next day Huanyao came to the mission house. Freddie Dun, one of the very strong Christian students, came with him. Millie got to talk and pray with Huanyao. He was, of course, very concerned about his mother. She and Freddie weren't sure at first what he understood personally about Jesus Christ, but at least they had tried to witness to him. He seemed comforted by their concern and prayers and by their promise to continue to pray for him.

Huanyao boarded the plane for the capital of Hunan province on Monday afternoon. From there, he was to catch a bus to his home town; however, at the bus station, he was told that the Communists now controlled all the roads outside of the capital. He could not get home. They said his best bet was to fly back out to Guilin. Huanyao didn't know what to do. He had spent most of his money flying there. He didn't have enough to buy a ticket. He walked back to the airport. He just stood there at the edge of the airfield trying to figure out what to do. He thought about his friends praying for him in Guilin. Maybe he could pray, too, if he only knew how. Finally he prayed, "Dear God, my friends in Guilin say that You are real and that You will help me when I need help. I don't know what to do. If You are there, will you help me now?"

Suddenly a hand grabbed his arm pulling him toward the plane on the runway. The person said, "Young man, if you are going to get on that plane, you are going to have to hurry." The person was now pulling his arm and running beside him.

A stewardess standing at the door of the plane exclaimed, "Hurry, hurry, we are just ready to take off."

The person pushed him up the stairs as the stewardess said, "Come in."

The person did not come in the plane with him and when Huanyao turned around to look for him, there was no one there. "Where is the man that was with me?" he asked the stewardess.

"What man? You were the only one on the airfield," she replied.

It gave him such a strange feeling. As soon as he sat down, the stewardess asked for his ticket.

"I don't have a ticket," he replied.

She was amazed, "You don't have a ticket? How did you get on this plane?"

"I don't know," he answered. "I guess God put me on this plane."

Since they were already taxiing down the runway, the stewardess said, "Well, you can't get off now."

She suggested he could buy a ticket when he got off in Luchow. Poor Huanyao didn't even know where the plane was going. Luckily he had an uncle in Luchow, and it was just one hundred miles south of Guilin. He could return to the university!

Millie heard this story because the very next Sunday Huanyao was back on campus in the Christian Fellowship meeting sharing this testimony. After just a few weeks, he did formally accept Christ as his personal Savior and was baptized in the church. He became a quiet, but steady Christian believer.

The students continued their studies until the summer vacation. By that time, the Communists had taken control of Guilin. The university students were scattered throughout China with no choice as to whether they would further their education or go back to their homes. They were sent where the government wanted them to go. Millie heard that Huanyao was eventually sent far north.

Millie never quit praying for Huanyao. She hoped some day to see him again. At the time of her death, she was planning another trip to China for May, 1996. She hoped to go by way of Vladivostok, Russia, entering China from the north Manchurian capital. Chinese friends had last heard that Huanyao lived near Harbin and they were trying to help her locate him.

Where Is Mommy? Where is Daddy?

There were so many sad things happening as the Communists took over Guilin. Millie especially felt sorry for the children. Here is one of the stories she related to me:

> One of our language teachers in Guilin spoke beautiful Mandarin but with a different accent. I found out he was from Mongolia. He was very tall, and quite handsome. The regular Southern Chinese are usually much shorter. He was married to a very attractive woman, and they had two sweet children.
>
> As the Communists came closer to Guilin, the government Nationalist people and the armed forces retreated. To our surprise and concern, this man's wife left her home and her family and went with them!
>
> When the Communists marched into the city, the Mongolian teacher came and welcomed them just like the other Chinese did. Everyone was very nervous, and tried to be friendly. After all, we were being "liberated". Within a week after the Communists came, the Mongolian teacher disappeared. We never had any news of him - never knew what had happened to him. We assumed he had been killed by the Communists.
>
> The two children didn't have a home; they didn't have anybody. They were just sort of on the streets. The little boy was about six and the little girl was about three-and-a-half.
>
> I can still picture in my mind this little boy holding his arm around his little sister; two little children against the world. It was so pathetic. Everyone was afraid to help the little ones because it might make the Communists

angry. We missionaries could be given our exit visas at
any time, so we could not provide any lasting care. At
last there was one Chinese couple who said, "We don't
care what happens to us. These children need help."
They went and got the children and took them into their
own home. I prayed for that couple and for the children,
that the Lord would give them a special blessing and
protect them.

After that, we didn't hear what happened to any of them.
Soon we were given exit visas and told to leave China. I
didn't understand how that mother could just leave them,
but in those days we saw many strange things. We will
never find out what happened to many Chinese until we
reach eternity.

Freddie

One of the best Christian friends that Millie had in Guilin was
Freddie Dun. Unlike most Chinese students, Freddie came from a
Christian home. His family lived near Shanghai where his father
was an Anglican Bishop in charge of several provinces in East
China. Millie never met the father personally, but she wrote to
him. He was known as a very wonderful Christian and an
impressive person. Freddie had a brother who was also a minister
and served in a Presbyterian church.

Freddie never felt called to be a full-time pastor or a Christian
worker, but he was always a faithful servant of God with high
ideals about life. When Millie met him, he was studying to be an
electrical engineer.

Millie could always count on Freddie in the Kwangsi
University Christian Fellowship. He kept up with the other
members of the group, witnessing to them and praying for them.
Millie especially remembered Freddie at one of the Spring
Conference prayer meetings praying for himself that "God would
keep him forever from the power of Satan." Freddie's life had
many hard times, but Millie felt this prayer was answered.

When the Communist forces took Guilin and sent students away from the colleges and also away from their homes, Freddie was sent to Shanghai - much closer to home than most students. Freddie's father, the Anglican Bishop, was taken to prison. Most of China's religious leaders met this fate in the next several years. Many were beaten, poorly fed, and unmercifully brainwashed. Later many were sent to work on collective farms. Freddie's brother, the Presbyterian minister, was also sent to prison. He *died* there which left his wife and his daughters alone.

During these hard years, Freddie was the one student in China who kept up with Millie and always knew where she was. She had a pretty good idea where he was too, although once they didn't write for almost ten years. He finally wrote, "It wasn't convenient" which meant it might be dangerous for Freddie. When Millie wrote, she used her Chinese name and did not identify herself as a foreigner. There was an active "grapevine" of information that passed from Chinese friends across the Bamboo Curtain into Hong Kong. Millie knew that Freddie found a Christian wife and they had three daughters.

During the Cultural Revolution, Freddie was very ill in the hospital. He wrote, "I am praying to God to make me well again, and to keep you well, until the day that we can meet again and clasp hands." God answered this prayer, and healed him.

Years later after Mao died, Premier Deng Xiaoping tried to turn back from the harsh treatments of the Red Guards and the worst of the revolutionaries. He realized that a lot of the imprisonment and tortures of the Chinese, especially of the Christian leaders, was unjustified. Premier Deng was a kinder, gentler man. Most Pastors and leaders were freed from prison and work camps. At last, Freddie's father was released, but they couldn't bring back the life of Freddie's brother. Officials gave his widow an interesting choice: "You can stay in China, or if you would rather leave, we will give you a passport to someplace else. What do you want to do?" She had a relative in New Zealand, so she and her daughters chose to emigrate there. China held too many bad memories for them.

Millie very quietly and cautiously joined a tour to Shanghai in 1978. She did not try to contact anyone. With her blond hair and strong Swedish features, she was hardly one who could disappear in a crowd of Chinese. She returned again in 1979 and felt more freedom for herself and also among the Chinese people. After she got back to Macau, she wrote to a few friends telling them that she had visited Shanghai. Immediately Freddie wrote back and said he wanted to see her on her next visit.

By 1980, she felt it was safe for her Chinese friends to actually meet her again and talk together. She told Freddie the hotel where she would be staying so he might meet her quietly there. Surprise! He and his wife, Tsun-Fong, and their three daughters met her at the airport. Millie remembered this important day - Monday, May 26, 1980 - the day that she and Freddie got to meet each other again and clasp hands. His wife and daughters were already calling her, "Aunt Millie", and Freddie said this was "... right and proper, for she is my sister."

Freddie had actively contacted the Christians in Shanghai who knew or who knew about Millie. Co-workers filled in at his job so that he could have three days free to accompany Millie to the homes of her Christian "young people", now 30 years older. C.K. Zhang came 200 miles by train to see Millie when his wife, who was traveling near Shanghai, told him Millie was coming.

Freddie, his family, and some friends took Millie to a fancy restaurant one night where Freddie openly, unfrightened and unashamed, offered a prayer to Almighty God in thanks. Two or three years earlier, this act surely would have gotten Freddie in big trouble, probably put in prison. His daughters, who had never been in a church in their lives, knew about Jesus and had grown up in a Christian home, right there in Communist China.

When Chinese were allowed to go to the newly-opened church in Shanghai, they immediately had a problem. The church capacity was 800 - the attendance was soon at 2,000! It was necessary to have three services in this "hungry-for-God" place.

Millie continued to visit Freddie and his family in Shanghai every time she had a chance to get near this city, and she introduced many of her friends and tour groups to this special friend and brother.

For Millie's retirement party in Hong Kong, Freddie and his family recorded a special tape praising God for knowing Millie and for having her as such a special friend. Then he invited all the other Christians in Shanghai to contribute to this special greeting. Very many did - some in Mandarin, some in English. Listening to the tape, a person might think that Millie's whole missionary career was spent in North East China; instead, she spent a little less than four short years in Guilin, South China, but she had faithfully continued to "follow her students".

Chapter Four

THE HONG KONG YEARS

When Millie finally got out of China, she spent several months in Hong Kong and Macau before she fully regained her health. She arrived in Hong Kong with amoebic dysentery and worms. When she was able to sail for a furlough in America, she was unsure where the mission board would reassign her since China was now closed. How thankful she was when a Chinese pastor in Hong Kong requested that she be sent as a youth worker to the Hong Kong Baptist Association. At least, she could serve close to China in this open port city on lease to Great Britain until 1997.

All Those Letters

Millie was already writing letters to many friends and relatives when she first went to Guilin. When she had to leave the city ... and China ... on October 31, 1950, she took with her the names and addresses of her new Chinese friends. She intended to write them as soon as she got to Hong Kong. Instead she ended up in the hospital with a siege of dysentery. In the tense atmosphere of Guilin, she hadn't even realized she was ill. During her stronger moments that winter, she wrote and sent books and other materials to help her Chinese friends in their adjustment to a Communist world.

In December, she moved to the Portuguese colony of Macau, three hours by boat from Hong Kong. Like Hong Kong, the area around Macau had been leased out by China; however, the Macau lease had been made in 1557 and it was made with Portugal instead of Great Britain. It lies about forty miles from Hong Kong across the wide mouth of the Pearl River where it flows into the South China Sea. With less of the pressure of international trade, it was a quieter place to regain her health, study, and write to friends behind the Bamboo Curtain. It was easier for Chinese friends to write to her in Macau since most of the population there was Chinese.

At Christmas time, she wrote 200 letters to nearly every Chinese friend that she knew and had a close acquaintance with during the last four years in China. She felt for some of them, "Perhaps mine was the only Christmas greeting they received. Maybe it won't be long before some of my friends won't be able to get any mail at all." She received many letters of joy and appreciation and prayer requests from Guilin friends.

In January and February, she wrote her "Christmas" letter to most of her stateside friends explaining why she hadn't gotten to them before, and asking for earnest prayers for her friends in China.

Millie always had letters to write. When she traveled, she carried a shoulder bag full of letters to be re-read and answered as soon as she had time. Why so many letters? It was an important part of her talent and her ministry of encouragement. Many of her missionary friends were amazed at all the people she continued to correspond with and they wrote about these things to me:

Missionary Dick Lusk said,

"In 1962, Millie lived in half of the big mission house in Macau. My wife, Ida, and I were in the other half, and I was traveling back and forth to Hong Kong. Millie was a night owl. Many were the nights when I would wake up at three or four A.M. to see her lights still on. Most of her letter writing was done in the early morning hours."

Missionary friend, Vi Marie Taylor, remembered,

"Soon after I was appointed a missionary associate to Hong Kong in 1977, I received a cordial letter from Millie, welcoming me to the field and briefing me on the Hong Kong/Macau Baptist Mission. One of the things

Millie told me was that she saw as part of her ministry, the writing of letters. As I got to know Millie, I felt that this was very true, but I would broaden that to include other types of communication, from personal visits to remote areas to uncovering for less-experienced missionaries some understanding of the people and culture of China."

As a young journeyman missionary from 1975-1977, Steve Baker worked under and with Millie. He said,

"She always had time for me, and invited me over for tea or a meal to catch up on how I was doing and to share personal matters and plan activities for the Chinese young people. Every time I was at her house, I would see her typewriter with piles of letters to answer and letters to mail and one or more in progress."

Missionary, Kathryn White, wrote,

"I was indeed fortunate to be able to make two trips into China with Millie. Millie had a lot of good traits and strengths, but probably the one that stands out the most to me was the way she 'held on' to people. To me she was a modern 'Paul'. Just as Paul wrote to encourage the new Christians in Bible times, Millie constantly wrote to China friends to encourage them to 'keep the faith' during some hard years under the Communists. It was such a joy to meet many of her former students as we traveled over China. I am sure she knew someone in every province."

Elizabeth Ward was another letter writer and a very special friend of Millie's. She was a Eurasian from Shanghai who had come to Hong Kong to work in the Baptist offices as Secretary of Foreign Missions. She had been a Sunday School teacher in Shanghai. Through the years, she continued to write to her Sunday School young people even as they were assigned to places far from Shanghai. It was a real shock to Millie when Elizabeth died. She knew that many of these young people, now adults, needed the Christian encouragement that Elizabeth's letters had brought.

Millie wrote to everyone in Elizabeth Ward's address book and told them about her death. She wrote that Elizabeth had been a very special friend of hers, and she knew she could never take her place, but she would like to at least be their friend. Elizabeth's Eurasian church in Shanghai had been English speaking, so Millie was able to write to them in English which made it much easier for her. Many did write back to her and became her pen-pal friends.

Millie had several address books - one for Hong Kong, one for Macau, one for China as well as for other parts of the world. There was one large book for the United States with the names listed alphabetically *under the state* they lived in. Even in America, many of the names were Chinese. She also had very many loose slips of papers and business cards of names and addresses that weren't in a book yet, with notations of who they were: "Evelyn and Katie's nephew; Jim - church member in Manila, Philippines; Joanne - met her in Pakistan, now in Minneapolis; a Bible woman who prayed for Martha for forty years; Emily - girl from Peking we met on the Yangtse River; Sylvia from West Germany - met in Lonzhou; Vorapieh at the Baptist Bookstore in Bankok, Thailand; a lady believer at the Catholic Church at Yichang; lady with a baby on a Guilin street; Roger - met in Calcutta", and so many, many more ... a nurse, a singer, a teacher, or a taxi driver from anywhere in the world.

Not only did Millie write to all these people, but Millie came from a large family who each regularly heard from her. She added bits of information about our news into her family letters. She kept us in touch with one another.

Nephew and niece, John and Edie Lovegren, were visiting her in Oregon for a week in the summer of 1986. John said two incidents brought home to them her vast number of friends and acquaintances. He said,

> We were discussing her prodigious correspondence and she was lamenting that, since moving back to the States, she had fallen increasingly behind in returning letters. She embarrassingly shared with us that she thought she probably owed letters to seven hundred friends. Seven

Hundred! Edie and I, after staring at one another in incredulous amazement, shared with her that, together, the two of us didn't even know seven hundred people, much less seven hundred to whom we had written a letter. Astounding!

Later in the week, we headed south to visit Crater Lake over the weekend. As our trip involved a Sunday, we located a Southern Baptist church in some obscure, small town in southern Oregon. After the service ended, we were exiting the sanctuary along with the one hundred or so other congregates. Aunt Millie rather sheepishly admitted that this was a rather strange experience for her. She just wasn't accustomed to not knowing *anybody* when attending a church service and it was rather odd not having some long-standing friendship to .... At about this point in her second sentence, some woman tapped her on the shoulder and said, "Are you Millie Lovegren, the missionary? When the guests introduced themselves, I just knew that name sounded so familiar. I've been praying for you for years! It's so good to finally meet you." So what else is new? She probably was added to the correspondence list.

The American Consul General

When Millie left Guilin, China, the new Communist government had made life hard for almost everyone. Her students were scattered throughout China. There were hate American campaigns that made witnessing for Christ almost impossible for Westerners. Missionaries were ordered out as soon as they received their exit visas. Millie was quite sick when she arrived in Hong Kong, and while she was recovering her health, she learned that Papa had been put in prison and mother was under house arrest in West China. The wonderful Dr. Bill Wallace, who served south of Guilin, died in prison. By the time Millie was well enough to travel home on furlough, she was discouraged. Several of her friends were going home on the same boat and hoped to cheer her up. Surprisingly, someone else came along to do that. Missionary friend, Fay Taylor, told about their departure for America in this way:

> We sailed on the presidential liner, the "President Cleveland", from Hong Kong to San Francisco. Many friends came to see us off. Besides Millie and me (Fay Taylor), Mrs. Hamlett and Marie Conner were also going home. "All ashore" had been called out. All the visitors had gone ashore and the gangplank had been raised for our departure. We took our places at the rail to wave goodbye to our well-wishing friends.
>
> Suddenly an announcement came over the loud speaker, "Miss Mildred Lovegren, please come to the main desk. Miss Lovegren ...." Millie hurried down to the main deck. Was there something wrong with her passport?
>
> The captain of the ship met her and took her to the gangplank that was being re-lowered. There she met the American Consul General. He had made a special visit to assure her that her father, Dr. Lovegren, would not be forgotten - that as long as he was in prison, the United States government would actively pursue his release, through all possible channels. He wanted her to assure the family at home that they were concerned for him. This was comforting to Millie. When the Consul General left, the gangplank was again raised, and we were on our way.
>
> One year later when Millie returned from furlough to Hong Kong, Dr. Lovegren was still in prison.

The United States Government did continue actively and through many channels to request Papa's release for over four-and-a-half years. At last, through arrangements made during the Geneva, Switzerland Conference in 1955, he was given an exit visa and sent out of China. I'm thankful that our United States government was concerned and vigilant in their determination to seek Papa's release. I'm even more thankful for the prayers of all the Christians on Papa's behalf that I feel influenced world affairs so that his release was possible and his mental and physical health were maintained. Thank You, God!

"The prayer of a righteous man is powerful and effective" (James 5:16b).

Theodosia

After Millie's first short term of service, it was almost impossible to measure any success at all. The college students she worked with were sent to jobs throughout China. Pastors and church leaders were in trouble for their faith, some even in jail. The work the missionaries had done was interpreted by the Communists as their way of pushing Western imperialism and power.

Many questions came to the minds of the missionaries. Why did this terrible thing happen? Could I have been a better missionary? Did I clearly teach people about God and about faith in Jesus? Did I understand enough to make good decisions? Do I have the necessary talents to be a missionary? Many questions remained as Millie returned from America to the British-owned colony of Hong Kong.

Sometimes when she talked to the older Chinese Christians, they referred to Theodosia Dean. Who??? "Theodosia! The wonderful missionary lady, who died in Hong Kong in 1843." 1843! Over a hundred years before! How and why did *anyone* know anything about her? What had made her so special? Millie determined to find out about this amazing missionary who died so long ago, and yet was still remembered with fondness by the Chinese people.

Millie learned that Theodosia was a seventeen-year-old English girl from Thetford, Norfolk, when she left England in 1835 to serve God in China. She may have been the first single, woman missionary. The trip was long and full of dangers as she sailed by herself around Africa, past India to Macau. At first she worked and lived with early German missionaries, Mr. and Mrs. Gutzslaffs. Then she worked with American Baptist missionaries from Virginia, Jay and Henrietta Shuck.

A few years before, the Shucks had traveled to the Orient with another couple, Mr. and Mrs. William Dean and their daughter, from Boston. These two couples stopped in Singapore where they were surprised to learn that there were several different Chinese languages. Mr. Dean started studying Swatow, and Mr. Shuck studied Cantonese. Tragedy struck when Mrs. Dean got sick and died there in Singapore. William Dean had to go on with his little daughter. They stopped for two or three weeks in Bangkok, where Mr. Dean discovered a large number of Swatow-speaking Chinese in the city. He and his little girl stayed in Bangkok while the Shucks traveled on to Cantonese-speaking Macau.

Every winter, Mr. Dean and his daughter went to visit their friends (the Shucks) in Macau where he often stayed with the Gutzlaffs. Mr. Dean had some trouble with the constant heat in Bangkok and found relief in the cooler Macau winters. During one of these visits, Mr. Dean met the new missionary, Theodosia Barker. After only one week, he proposed marriage to her. It took her two more weeks to accept. They married, and Theodosia returned with William Dean and his little daughter to Bangkok. This teenage girl from England, who now knew some German and Cantonese, had to start learning Swatow Chinese and Thai (Siamese).

Theodosia was not a Baptist. While studying her Bible as she worked with the Shucks, she wondered about baptism and continued searching her Bible to find out about it. When the first Swatow converts were baptized in Bangkok, the new Mrs. Dean was baptized with them. The Deans' married life was short, and there were many trials. Mr. Dean's health was often poor. He was gone a great deal of the time. They had a little boy, Edmund, who lived just over a year. The next year, 1842, they had a little daughter, Fanny, who was less than a year old when her mother, Theodosia, died of small pox on her 24th birthday. She had served God as a missionary for less than eight years. She had actually only been in Hong Kong for seven months, yet people there remembered her still.

Millie, as a single missionary, could imagine some of the things Theodosia had faced, and she was challenged by her dedication and sincerity, but what made her great? She didn't start a school, a church, or a clinic. Mainly she just taught the Bible and talked to people about God. The Chinese explained, "She had such a deep love for the Lord and for people." *Love for God and for people!* Was that the main talent a missionary needed? How simple! How profound!

On her next furlough, Millie journeyed to England before she returned to the United States. She went to Theodosia's "home church" in Thetford, England. She wanted to tell them about the young missionary who had felt God calling her to go from their church to China. She wanted the congregation to know that even though this happened before they were born, Theodosia's brief life was so filled with love for God and for people that her testimony was still influencing people today. Millie included!

> *"So faith, hope, and love abide, these three, but the greatest of these is love. Make love your aim"* (I Corinthians 13:13, 14:1a).

Teacher And Friend

Recognizing her gift of working with young people, Millie was assigned by the Hong Kong mission to teach in various schools and to work with the Youth Center. For several years, she taught classes in Old Testament one school year and New Testament the next in the Mandarin language at Baptist College. The class was especially for refugee students but also for those who spoke Cantonese and wanted to better understand the official language of China. She said about this class,

> All through the years I have never quite gotten over that *I had to leave China;* I had to leave students behind and I didn't really know what happened to them. So, if I could do something for mainland students, it made me feel like I was continuing the ministry that I had in the beginning.

There were usually too many students to get well-acquainted with any of them. One class had 107 students! She enjoyed being with the young people, but she did not always enjoy the time it took to prepare lessons and grade papers. While most missionaries would consider teaching as their missionary work, teaching sometimes interfered with what Millie most wanted to do - really get acquainted with the students and their families. In fact, she sometimes preferred to take college classes so that she could be a fellow student.

One incident that Donna Kirby relates shows Millie's heart for her students. Donna wrote:

> One day I received a letter in the mail that included a photo of a Chinese young man and Millie. I recognized the young man as a former student in Henrietta School, where I taught. I did not really remember that much about the student, just that I had taught him Bible in the twelfth grade; he was not one who really stood out in my memory.
>
> In the letter, he explained that Millie had just visited him in England where he was studying. I did not know that he knew Millie. I later learned that she had taken a great interest in the whole family, and had a part in their becoming Christians. She made a point of visiting him in England to continue to encourage him, and inspired him to write me the letter with the photo thanking me for teaching him.
>
> This story illustrates one of Millie's greatest strengths . . . personal involvement in many individual lives to point them to Christ, and to continue to nurture and encourage them in the faith.

Millie loved to take students on Christian retreats and camping experiences where she could really get acquainted with them. She encouraged students to meet other Christians and to attend Baptist Youth meetings throughout Asia and the world. She often used her own money, and gifts Americans sent her, to buy plane or boat tickets so that her young people could attend these international conferences; in so doing, many became Christian leaders, not only in Hong Kong but in many other countries.

During Millie's first year back in the Orient, Mother, who had been under house arrest for one- and-a-half years, was released and got out of China into Hong Kong. Papa was still detained in prison in Chungking. Mother did not wish to return to the United States even for a furlough. She wanted to be close in case Papa should be released. She lived with Millie for three years until Papa was set free. Since Mother also spoke Mandarin, she started working with the many poor refugees from mainland China. During this time, Millie became interested in the many stateless people in both Hong Kong and Portuguese Macau - refugees who had escaped into Hong Kong, who had no passports and, therefore, no country to claim as home.

Of course, Millie didn't work only with students and refugees; in fact, she had the privilege of becoming a deaconess in the Hong Kong Baptist Church. At that time, she was the only Caucasian on the board. I don't know if they have had any since. I think they considered her to be Chinese. She felt greatly honored to be chosen.

A College Witness

Millie was concerned that there seemed to be no Christian witness at Hong Kong University. There were surely plenty of students. Many had escaped from China. Other missionaries told Millie that the University had not been encouraging to Christians.

Millie decided to enroll as a student. She did not like to do anything undercover so she made an appointment with the head of the History Department. She told him she was a missionary and she wanted to audit an Ancient Chinese History course so she could learn more about China and get acquainted with some of the students. She hoped she could tell some of them about Christianity.

What do you know! The professor was not a Buddhist. He was a Baptist! He encouraged her, but said it would probably be better if she were in the smaller second-year course. She agreed.

Hong Kong University students - Chinese History Class (1955)

The first day in class, she was surprised to see a young girl she recognized and who she knew attended one of the Chinese Baptist churches. The girl was even more surprised to see Millie. She said that she felt God wanted her to start a Bible Study and prayer group on campus, but she told God she was afraid and she wouldn't do it unless He sent her a strong Christian student to help her. Millie was the answer to her prayers.

The girl was a good witness, and she soon found five other Christians who were willing to join in a Bible Study and prayer group. By the spring of her senior year, there were 125 college young people attending the group meetings. They had planned and carried out several summer and holiday retreats. Many of their friends had accepted Christ.

The Chinese girl hoped to spend her whole life serving Christ. She did - but it was a very short life. Before graduation, she died of a disease she had contracted before she had left China.

> "Only one life, 'twill soon be past.
> Only what's done for Christ will last."

First Communion

One day Millie took a new friend, Sophia who had recently come from Shanghai, to the Kowloon English church service. It was Sophia's first time in church although she had been a member of an underground (house) church in China for many years. The meeting was led by a deacon who was himself originally from Shanghai and was a good friend of Elizabeth Ward. The service was very worshipful, and Sophia followed it as best she could, though she was too new for her "listening English" ability to be adequate. She *could* read the Scripture around which the sermon was based.

The Lord's Supper was conducted at the close of the service. There was no remark that believers of other church groups were not welcome to partake. Millie turned to Sophia and told her she could take the elements or not take them as she wished. Sophia whispered that she had eaten breakfast (twenty years before as a child she had attended a Catholic Church, but hadn't understood). Millie told her that eating, or not eating breakfast was not important since all are unworthy to partake, but as we ask God's forgiveness, His grace makes us worthy to come to His table. She took the bread.

When when the grape juice was passed, she said, "What is this?"

Millie whispered, "Baptists believe that all are equal at the foot of the cross. The priest, as well as the people, are sinners saved by His grace. Baptists believe that the elements, the bread and the juice, do not change, but are to be taken to remember Jesus Christ's great gift to all."

Sophia said the service meant a great deal to her. It meant a lot to Millie, too, as she thought about taking the Lord's Supper with someone who had been a member of the underground church in China for over fifteen years without ever having the opportunity to take Communion.

Millie's Hong Kong

With no possibility of going back into Communist China, Millie was very happy to be reassigned to the Hong Kong and Macau mission where she could stay close to China. Hong Kong was an international trade center under the British government. English was used in government transactions and often in the business and educational fields. Aside from the Cantonese language problem, Millie found living in Hong Kong easy after the tense times in China. It was a rich city with many, many skyscrapers, and also a city with many poor refugees. She enjoyed showing new missionaries and visitors around the Crown Colony. Many of her friends had unusual experiences with Millie that they shared with me.

When new missionary, Katherine White, arrived in Hong Kong in 1959, she lived with Millie and Jaxie Short for about six months. She said,

> The very first week, Millie invited me to accompany her on a trip to Rennes Mills, a place in the New Territories where Chinese refugees had settled. I was surprised when Millie had us buy our lunch from a man on the road (cha-siu-pau ... steamed bread with barbecued meat). Was it clean?
>
> We visited several friends Millie knew from her China days, and we stayed so long that we missed the last bus back to Hong Kong Island. This didn't phase Millie. We simply walked to the beach where there was an inlet from the sea. She hired a small sampan to take us across to Clearwater Bay where we could catch a bus home. I was a little frightened during the sampan ride, but Millie seemed to think it was a natural way to travel when it was so late that regular transportation was not available.

Ida Lusk tells about "little hands":

> In 1963 at about 10:00 P.M. New Years Eve, Millie called and invited me to go with her to the flower market. I agreed and asked her when. Millie told me we should wait until almost midnight! She laughed at my surprise and said, "I'll be by to get you at 11:30. That should give us enough time to get there at midnight when they lower their prices, and the Chinese crowds really start shopping in earnest."
>
> When Millie arrived, she advised me not to take any money in my pockets. That was good advice. That night I learned the Chinese word for thief or pickpocket (siu shau = little hand). By the time we had returned home, many "little hands" had been inside my pockets. Never before had I seen such crowds all smiling and laughing in the festive spirit of the season while jostling each other about, seeking the best buys on flowers.

Millie took cousin, June Bruce, to a feast that she remembers like this:

In both 1962 and 1965, I came back home from Ethiopia through the Orient to visit Millie. During the second visit, some Christian Chinese were opening a flashlight factory and some Southern Baptists were invited to the open house along with other guests. There were perhaps 500 people there and, of course, it was all in Chinese. I sat between Millie and another American missionary while they interpreted and Millie told me what the different foods were and whether she thought I would like them. She advised me that I probably wouldn't like the abalone and duck feet dish. It was interesting that every time some food came to the tables that had duck in it, they all raised their glasses of orange drink in a toast.

My own daughter, Faith Keller, got to visit Aunt Millie and she related,

My husband, Phil, and I have very special memories of the time we visited Aunt Millie in 1974 in Hong Kong and Macau. She took us through settlement houses where folks were living as close as sardines, through whole villages in the city made of cardboard houses, and villages of boat houses on Chinese junks, some of which had TV antennae on their roofs.

We went to the border to see the gate where Grandpa Lovegren had crossed over to freedom when he was released by the Communists. We saw beautiful, green, open areas in the New Territories, and more boat villages in the harbor.

One particular place of great interest to me was in Kowloon. Aunt Millie led us through a doorway and down a flight of stairs into an underground city! It was poorly lit. The pathway had to be watched carefully as a sewage ditch ran alongside. This took some maneuvering as we passed people with large bundles. Aunt Millie was a calm, assured guide as we stepped over people in the pathway sleeping off their opium-induced stupor. Aunt Millie calmly informed us that one particularly harmless sleeper we stepped over was a much feared and vicious man when awake. Comforting thought!

Fay Taylor remembered "those yummy doughnuts". She said,

> My Chinese dialect was Mandarin. Millie was raised in
> Mandarin Chinese and had spoken it in Guilin, but in
> Hong Kong and Macau, the primary Chinese dialect is
> Cantonese which she studied hard to acquire when she
> was stationed there. One evening, Millie and I went to a
> Hong Kong Baptist Convention Meeting. On the way to
> the church, we passed a Russian bakery where large
> lovely doughnuts were on display in the window. We
> wanted to stop and try them, but our duty called, and we
> went on to the meeting. Most of the meeting was in
> Cantonese, so I missed a lot of what was going on.
> Sometimes Millie would whisper to me some of the
> important discussions or decisions. As the meeting drug
> on and I was feeling rather weary, Millie leaned toward
> me and whispered, "I'm still thinking about those
> doughnuts."
>
> This convention meeting, like most, had people coming
> and going. After a few more minutes of close attention
> to the proceedings, we took our leave and headed toward
> the Russian doughnut shop. Doughnuts are a treat in
> Asia, and they never tasted so good!

We Had Company

Yes, Millie had learned early that missionaries should be
hospitable. Often the rest of us were not so well conditioned to this
fact, but we learned. Missionary, Marie McKay, explained it this
way,

> I shared an apartment with Millie in 1962-1963. At
> times it was difficult since Millie did a lot of her work in
> the evenings and at night. I worked all day at the college
> and at the seminary, so our schedules were hard to mesh
> ... and we had company! Millie's parents spent a month
> with us during that year. Her cousin, Franklin Nelson,
> who had just been made head of the Baptist General
> Conference Mission Board, visited us on his way home

from Burma, where he had been a missionary. Several single women missionaries from Taiwan, or those passing through to other fields, stopped and stayed some days with us. Sam, my husband to be, came to visit. He stayed with the Morgans on the second floor, but he ate with us. Someone was always coming or going.

I love the story that Fay Taylor told:

Millie was very generous and given to hospitality. She invited people in for a cup of tea, a meal, a night, or for a vacation. She also invited people to the homes of her friends. For instance, one morning in Hong Kong I was told by my Amah, "There is a dark woman sleeping in the guest bed."

"Who is she?" I asked.

Seo Leen did not know her, but she told me that Miss Millie had brought her to our apartment at about midnight, after I had already retired. As I was eating breakfast, the "dark lady" in a sari dress came down the hall. She looked at me, and I looked at her. We had never seen each other before. I said, "Good morning," and she responded, and then went to the bathroom. When she came back by the dining room, I asked her to have some breakfast. She sat down, and we introduced ourselves. She was passing through Hong Kong and needed a bed for the night. Millie knew her from a visit to India, or some conference they had attended. She had met her at the airport the night before and brought her to my apartment. I don't know where Millie slept, or if she returned at that hour to Macau.

The Indian lady left soon after breakfast to continue her journey. I never saw her again. She was a Christian sister who Millie had helped along the way.

Cousin, John Skoglund, said,

During the year I taught at the Chinese University and at Baptist Seminary in Hong Kong, we discovered what a truly great missionary Millie was. She was utterly fearless. Both Chinese and missionary colleagues had great respect for her. She was in our home many times. In fact, we never knew when she was coming; so we fixed up a cot in our youngest daughter's room ready for Millie. Sometimes it was one A.M. when our bell rang ... and there was Millie. She had taken the last ferry from Macau where she lived and worked, and probably did not want to disturb anyone else. After all, we were related.

A Trip To Borneo

Missionary, Marie McKay, had an interesting trip with Millie. She said,

I met Millie for the first time on September 30, 1959, when I, along with Elaine Hancock, arrived in Hong Kong on the S.S. President Cleveland. Elaine and I were assigned to live at 167 Boundary Street, third floor, with Kathryn White who had arrived six months earlier. Millie and Jaxie Short lived at 169 Boundary, third floor. They had arranged with the mission to cut a door in the divider on the porch so that it would be easy to pass back and forth from one apartment to another. Both Jaxie and Millie were our friends and guides, as well as our transportation since they both were assigned cars, while the three of us were not assigned a car until we finished two years of language study.

My first long trip with Millie came in the summer of 1960. Millie asked if anyone would go with an Association group and her on a trip to Taiwan. I agreed to go. However, the shipping company would not let foreigners travel deck passage which is what the group planned to do. After that, Millie felt she had to find a trip for the two of us, so she was quite excited to find a Norwegian freighter going from Hong Kong to Bangkok, a ten-day round trip, and at a price we could afford. So we booked the trip.

Arriving in Bangkok, we found that the freighter had freight for Borneo, and if we stayed on the boat, our ticket covered until they arrived back in Hong Kong.

They would refund the smaller half of the ticket if we wished to return some other way. I did not have any more money to finish buying the air ticket and Millie was, as usual, short of cash so we decided to take the long way home.

At the first stop, Labuan, Millie and I looked up the Anglican pastor, a Chinese man. Millie asked if any missionaries were located on the north rim of Borneo, as we were to make several stops. The pastor said he didn't know any missionaries, but gave us the name of a man at the bank that was the "friend of missionaries". We went to the bank and did find him to be truly "the friend of missionaries", knowing all of them in the whole territory. A family and some single missionaries from Brunei were vacationing at the beach in Labuan and, in fact, were in town. He sent someone out to find them, and introduced them to us. He gave us the names of people in other ports, and Millie wrote them notes telling of our arrival. In Jessleton, we met Geoffrey Bull who had been in prison with her Dad, and we met his wife and little children. He was the interim pastor of a Brethren church. A New Zealand Baptist family who worship with the Brethren group, took us on Monday morning to a nearby island where shells cluttered the beach. At Tawau, the Anglican pastor, his family, and the school principal entertained us. The pastor took us to call on the Karen Woodcutters who had come from Burma to work. Since there was no Baptist work, this pastor felt a responsibility to minister to them. We met another couple, the old father of a man who had been a missionary in China, and Millie knew of him, and they knew several people in common.

When we returned to Hong Kong, Millie wrote a report on her observations and sent them on to the Foreign Mission Board. In the following years, the Malaysian Mission sent people to begin work in most of those places we had visited.

A Place to Serve

After World War II, our whole family had spread out in different directions. We had no Lovegren's left in Alabama, but we had special friends of our parents at Howard College, Dr. Vernon and Marjorie Davison. They became our family and especially Millie's home and headquarters when she was anywhere near Alabama on furloughs.

One day when Millie was running late as usual, and the Davisons were literally pushing her on the train, Millie said, "I spend so much time in your home, why don't you come to see me?"

Vernon answered her, "Get me a place to teach, and we will come."

What a foolish thing to say to Millie! She could always find a place for anyone who was willing to serve. She had barely landed in Hong Kong before Vernon started getting information from several colleges as far away as India. Before this, the Davisons had not realized Millie's intense interest in India. When the country broke up into two nations and later into three - India, Pakistan and Bangladesh - the acute refugee problems had bothered Millie so much that she had seveal times asked the Foreign Mission Board to allow her to go to India for short periods, up to three months. She also was concerned about the problems of Serampore College near Calcutta. They constantly needed trained faculty members, even for one semester. Millie tried to influence many of her professor friends to give a half a year to India.

So in 1962, Vernon took a sabbatical leave from Samford University in Birmingham to teach theology for one semester at Serampore college. Marjorie, a school teacher, also taught classes. It was difficult for them to believe the extreme poverty of the Indian people. A man could work all day in a mill and earn only one rupee (approximately twenty cents in U.S. currency). A national with a master's degree who taught in college, earned about $60 a month. What a learning experience for them!

By the Spring of 1963, Millie had arranged for the Davisons to teach at Hong Kong Baptist College. Even at a Baptist school, only about 25% of the students came from Christian homes! Since Bible was a required course, teachers were able to talk about Christ in any class. They could also witness anytime, even visiting their students' homes to talk to their non-Christian families.

Vernon was sure there were Communists in his classes. They often made a practice of entering various schools and investigating Western teachings. They listened quietly and never asked questions or participated orally.

Millie was very happy to have Vernon and Marjorie in her part of the world, and to have them teaching and working with students. What fun to have these "family members" sharing in her work.

In June when the school term was done, it was again time for Millie's furlough. The Davisons joined her as she traveled home the *long way*, visiting missionary and Christian friends in Thailand, Burma, East and West Pakistan, Egypt, Jordan, Syria, Lebanon, Greece, Italy, Switzerland, France, Holland, Denmark and England! When traveling with Millie to visit friends, one *could* get a world tour.

Vernon and Marjorie were not the only family members that ended up serving in either or both India and Hong Kong. Niece, Dr. Edie Lovegren, worked in a hospital in India, and cousins, Dr. John and Daisy Skoglund taught in both countries.

The Old Rice Pot

One day after Papa got out of prison in China, he and Millie were walking in Hong Kong near a construction zone where hills were being flattened to make room for new housing developments. Millie saw a child running down the street with some strange little images sometimes found in tombs. The child came up to a police officer and asked, "Would you like to buy it?" as he held up a little house.

"Where did you get that?" the policeman inquired.

The child pointed to the construction site, and he said, "There are a lot more inside."

The busy workers had inadvertently opened an old unknown tomb entrance. Construction was stopped until archaeologists could examine, and remove the artifacts. Experts from the University in Hong Kong dated the articles at around 2,000 years old. Under a great deal of pressure from the local people, the government stopped the idea of apartments and turned the old burial site into a park.

Before the artifacts were properly cataloged and sent to a museum, they were put on display for the local people who had witnessed all these events. Papa and Millie were interested, too, especially since they had been in on the original child's discovery. As they were looking around, Papa noticed an old jar, or rice pot, about the size of a large mixing bowl. He called it string pottery, and felt that it was even older than 2,000 years. How did Papa know about such things? I don't know. He was curious, and he read a lot. He use to say he didn't have a photographic memory just a "sticky" mind. Anyway, Millie particularly noticed the pot.

A few years later on a vacation trip to Thailand, Millie and a friend were riding on a little flat boat near the ancient capital of Siam. Several boats in the center of the river were fishing with nets, not for fish, but for pottery and other things that they could sell. Millie noticed at the bottom of one of the boats an old unbroken rice pot. It looked like string pottery.

"Let's buy some pottery," Millie said to her friend.

"What do you want?" she asked, and was surprised when Millie answered, "I want that pot that is on the floor of that boat."

"Why?" questioned the friend. After all, the old pot wasn't colorful or particularly pretty like some of the other pieces.

"Because I think it is old," Millie replied.

Their boat drifted to the floating market where Millie got the pot and her friend bought some pretty items. "If it is old," the friend reminded her, "you will not be allowed to take it out of Thailand."

"O.K.," Millie said. "If it is old, and I cannot take it out, I will give it to you; but if I can, I will take it to Hong Kong."

She paid only the equivalent of about $2.30 in American dollars.

When Millie was getting ready to return to Hong Kong, she explained to the customs officers in Bangkok where she had bought it and how much it cost. She left it with them for evaluation. Four or five months later, one of the Thai missionaries who was traveling to Hong Kong, brought the pot to Millie. The Customs Officials said it was only 60 or 70 years old so there was no problem in taking it out of Thailand. Millie was happy to get it, but she was sure it was much older.

Millie brought it to Hong Kong University where professors examined it and excitedly said it was at least 1,000 years old. They declared it to be stamp pottery, and to definitely be Chinese.

"If you put your hand in the jar you will feel a handprint inside," they explained.

Millie had never tried that. They said that as the artisan made the jar, one hand would remain in place inside, while the other hand would stamp the outside.

On her next furlough, Millie brought the pot to America and as she visited her family and friends, she also visited local museums. We, her sister and family, lived in Kansas City at that time. I was with Millie as we took the pot to the Nelson Art Gallery. The antiquities curator there was very interested and wanted Millie to loan it to the Gallery for display. She declined.

She carried it all over the United States and also to England. She loaned it to the Museum of History in Hong Kong for three years and later had it in Taiwan. When Millie retired, she reclaimed the pot, and brought it home to the United States. It has been dated from 60 to 70 years old by the Thailand Customs Officials to 3,000 years before Christ.

Mother was always disgusted at these side ventures that Millie could become interested in.

"What are you dragging that old pot around for? Forget the pot and preach the gospel," she said.

Actually the pot gave Millie many opportunities to talk to people with whom she normally would not have come in contact, like museum curators.

Millie said she never got all the answers about the pot that she wanted, but that it had opened up a whole new list of questions about the movement of people. The fact that this old Chinese jar was found in Thailand certainly suggests that there were people traveling between China and Thailand at the time of Christ. And even in that first century, travelers might have brought the news of Christ to China.

A Car From Lottie Moon

Millie really appreciated her little car, and she was very thankful for the generous Lottie Moon offerings that were taken every Christmastime for foreign missions. That made it possible for missionaries to have cars. She wrote this article to express her thanks:

Nellie Belle, my little green Volkswagen, has had a busy day. She really isn't mine. She actually came from the Lottie Moon Offering. I wonder if that good lady could ever have dreamed of the blessings she would bring to missionaries and to Christ's kingdom in 1965 when she wrote that letter in 1887 suggesting an offering at Christmastime for Foreign Missions.

The little green car has had several drivers. At first she raced long distances between chapels in the New Territories - to the Hong Kong Baptist Theological Seminary in Kowloon and then home on Hong Kong Island. Ronald Fuller was at the wheel. Then Mack, L.G. McKinney, took over and our little car shortened her path. She found her way almost daily to and from Pui Ching Middle School, but adventure still beckoned as Nellie Belle began making an ever increasing number of side trips on behalf of a beginning Colony-wide Music Program.

Mack and Flo left for America and Nellie Belle was still with us. This time she changed languages as Charles Cowherd drove her from Mandarin Church to Mandarin Chapel. She was serving now the refugee friends from Mainland China. Yet Nellie Belle was not working exclusively with Mandarin speaking people those days. Charles Cowherd was running an informal Baptist Mission Tour Service for many "Christians Passing Through", mission-minded sailors and some miscellaneous "Cotton Pickin' Tourists".

Then another car-swap brought Nellie Belle, now more grey than green, unresistingly into my hands when I returned to Hong Kong from furlough in America. Yes, Nellie Belle was old, but she had a lot of fight in her yet.

It has been Sunday today. Nellie Belle made two trips before Sunday School carrying seven blind young people, plus two little girls and a missionary friend (Elaine Hancock) to church. Two of the blind youth with respective little sisters, we picked up beside their homes. Five came from a school for the blind sponsored by a gracious German Lutheran group. After the morning worship service, we drove these five school youths back to their school while the other two joined Elaine in the monthly Business Meeting of the Caine Road Baptist Church. I returned to find the church members standing for the closing prayer. To my joy, I learned that the church had just voted to give regular monthly support to the Hong Kong Baptist Student Center - a new effort for

Hong Kong Baptists and many hours of my week are spent there. Nellie Belle did not pause long. With the two blind girls and their sisters safely deposited back at their homes, Elaine and I crossed the harbor by vehicular ferry to the city of Kowloon where we shared a delightful lunch with Juliette Mather and Jaxie Short in the sea-view dining room on the top of the Ambassador Hotel.

Time was still pressing. Our meal just over, Nellie Belle nervously made her way deep into Kowloon to pick up Chinese friends in a Swatow language chapel. We were to go to the ground-breaking service for a new Swatow Baptist Church in Kun Tong, a satellite town on the eastern edge of the Kowloon Peninsula. I was ten minutes late and wondered if the folk would have waited for me. The Lord helped us. Though the friends had left the chapel, their bus had not yet arrived. Miss Chen saw Nellie Belle come chugging along. The ground-breaking was exciting - a beautiful piece of land surrounded by thousands of homes, one of the larger resettlement estates of the Colony. After the service, Nellie Belle carried us up the hill to the home of missionaries Alvin and Barbara Koons, American Baptists from Kansas.

After a delightful tea-fellowship, it was time to return to Kowloon to pick Elaine up to return to vesper services on Hong Kong Island. Nellie Belle returned Miss Chen and her Swatow friends to their home base in Brotherly-Love Village. Then soon thereafter, Elaine and I were again on the ferry bound for Victoria City on Hong Kong Island. We were amused to be followed on and off the ferry by the Logan Templeton family in another Lottie Moon car. Firmly on land again, we ladies stopped briefly at my home just above the Baptist Student Center and then started to our evening opportunities.

Nellie Belle dropped Elaine off at the Hong Kong English Language Church where the Templetons had also been bound. Elaine would later return to her home in the New Territories with them. Very soon she, too, will be mobile in her own Lottie Moon car. Elaine

Hancock is head nurse at Hong Kong Baptist Hospital and has only recently returned from furlough.

Nellie Belle now retraced her path to pick up Sheila Lau, one of the blind girls, again. Sheila was baptized on Easter Sunday and the New Members Class is still in progress. Church folk would see that she returned home safely for Nellie Belle's day was not yet concluded. Twenty minutes later found the little green-grey car parked near the North Point Mandarin Baptist church. The service there presented in a language close to my heart and easy on my ears, brought rest and refreshment to a rather weary lady missionary. The service was over and Nellie Belle's driver found that she could still move across Victoria for a brief, late visit to Queen Mary Hospital where a dear missionary friend, Cornelia Leavell, was recovering from back surgery.

The day was finally over. Nellie Belle had little gas left in her and moved home rather hoarsely. It had been a long, busy, but wonderful day for the little car and her driver. Of course, Lottie Moon could not have visualized such a varied witness for one day because folk moved in mule-carts in her day. Nellie Belle's driver thanks Lottie Moon's modern friends and co-workers who have prayed and given generously to the Lottie Moon Christmas Offering. Thus, this little old car has been able to provide such an opportunity of witness in Hong Kong, and now because of your gifts this year Nellie Belle is being permitted to retire - a nice, strong, new Ford Cortina is soon to come to take her place.

Culture Shock

My daughter-in -law, Evelyn Lambert, related,

Most of the time when Aunt Millie came home on furlough, she had a period of time when she experienced culture shock. The early 70's was a time of many shocks and difficult times, I'm sure. One of the obvious contrasts was the prosperity of the United States in comparison with the rest of the world. But at the same time, one of the growing spiritual 'fads' was a 'wealth/health' or 'name it/claim it' teaching. Accompanying this teaching was the implication that, if you were sick, it was because you didn't have enough faith; if you were not prospering, you must not be praying right or something was wrong in your spiritual walk.

On furlough soon after Millie arrived in the U.S., we were together at a family gathering of some sort. She commented on this current teaching and some of the problems she had with it. Particularly as she had just traveled through India and, I believe, Nagaland on her way home and they were in the midst of a very serious and long drought.

She told of the Christians she had talked with and knew. Were they experiencing drought because they had poor faith? She didn't think so.

One of the Christian men in India told her, "If the Lord feeds us (he and his family), we will live. If He doesn't, we will die."

As she told it, it seemed to me that this was a much more powerful testimony of faith than those who could only see faith in prosperity. I have meditated on this brief story many times through the years. This man and his family would continue to follow the Lord, no matter what the circumstances. He would not compromise his faith by stealing, even to feed his family, trying to provide for them himself. In the years since, as I have had a family of my own, I have been able to appreciate even more the burden and temptation this could be.

One of the many gifts Millie brought to us were the windows to the world, especially in her stories of her Christian friends. I saw the reality of being family with believers around the globe - some growing with much to teach us, and some, too, that were learning in their walk with Christ just like we're learning.

Chapter Five

THE MACAU YEARS

In 1966, the awful Cultural Revolution and the Red Guards were spilling over the borders of China into Hong Kong and Macau. Both little countries had strikes, riots, and bomb scares, but the tension was worst in Macau. Chinese propaganda blared from radio loudspeakers constantly. Priemier Mao pictures were placed in buses, public places and schools - even the Baptist schools!

The Mission Board asked all missionaries to move to the safer Hong Kong which they gladly did. Two men missionaries and Millie continued to commute one or two days a week to teach in the Baptist school. She said she taught right under Mao's picture. Only a gatekeeper was left at the mission compound. In 1968 when things got a little better, Millie hoped that some missionaries would return to Macau, but none did.

When Millie returned from furlough in 1970, the mission house in Macau was still unused. Millie asked the Board to let her move to Macau - after all, Southern Baptists had lots of missionaries in Hong Kong and none in Macau where they had worked for 60 years. Millie's lady servant, Ah Hang, was willing to go with her. The Board reluctantly agreed because Millie was single and only responsible for her own life.

Two or three times she was in danger from the rioting. Missionary friend, Eleanor Tate, relates this incident:

> During the years of the Cultural Revolution in Red China, Red Guards would surge across the border into Macau and Hong Kong. During one of these occasions, Millie was touring a journalist friend around Macau in a taxi. It was the infamous day when the Red Guards were

making the British High Commissioner stand bare-headed all day in the sun to humiliate him. Of course, the journalist couldn't miss this chance to get pictures of the event. As soon as he started snapping photos, the Red Guards surrounded their taxi.

Millie, always quick to act immediately, took charge and told the journalist, "Give them the film." She helped him rip it out of the camera, and she handed it to the belligerent gang and said in Mandarin, "There, you have the film." Then she ordered the terrified taxi driver, "Drive on," speaking to him, of course, in Cantonese. She got them out of there before the Red Guards had time to react. Because of occasions like this, many of Millie's friends declared she was utterly fearless.

Millie had a dream for Macau. She wanted the missionaries to come back. She requested teachers, a doctor and a nurse, a social worker to help with the refugees, a youth worker, a pastor from Brazil to help the Portuguese, a Burmese pastor, an English-speaking pastor and many more. As it became more peaceful and while Millie was still on the field, she saw most of these needs met.

Steve Baker, who had been a two-year journeyman working with students in Macau under Millie's leadership, wrote:

Millie retired from the Foreign Mission Board in 1985, and I returned as a career missionary in 1986. By that time, there were about fifteen missionaries here. I heard one of the Chinese local Baptists remark about Millie, "They had to send fifteen missionaries to take her place."

Millie's Macau

Macau, like Hong Kong, is an international port city leased from China by the Portuguese. It will revert back to China in 1999. It is a very historical city known for its churches and its gambling - the Las Vegas of the Orient. It was from here that Christianity got its modern start in China. The old Protestant

Cemetery is the final resting place of people who came from all corners of the earth, including Dr. Robert Morrison who compiled the first English and Chinese dictionary and translated the Bible into Chinese.

When missionary, Fay Taylor, moved to Hong Kong from Indonesia, Millie had a close friend as well as a co-worker helping her. Fay enjoyed so many of the same things Millie did. She talked about Macau in this way,

> In our many walks about Macau, Millie and I loved to visit old historic places, the most famous is just a block from the mission compound - the ancient facade of the old St. Paul's Cathedral with the cross still standing on the top. It was said that Governor John Bowring was inspired to write the hymn, "In the Cross of Christ I Glory, Towering O'er the Wrecks of Time", when he steamed into the harbor, and looked up at the one wall of the church left standing. The cathedrals, the old forts, the temples all were interesting to us. The old Protestant Cemetery is fascinating with the English names of the heroes of the East India Company. It is the burial place of Robert Morrison and his family. Millie liked taking visitors to these places.

St. Paul's facade - note the cross at the very top.

St. Paul's was built by refugees in the 17th century
and struck by lightning and burned in the 18th century.

She and I enjoyed meals in many of the quaint and
interesting restaurants of Macau; sidewalk cafes, Chinese
tea houses, the old Colonial Hotel, and the modern
Lisbon Hotel. We liked the buns from the big, old
Portuguese ovens nearby.

Millie introduced me to many interesting and sometimes
important people - the wife of the highest Portuguese
judge, the Macanese lady next door, the Catholic priest
who taught at the Catholic Seminary and was a noted
writer and historian, the crippled Chinese lady who
seldom got out of her house, and the mother-less students
far from home. We were invited to dine in homes of the

other missionaries, in Chinese homes, in Indonesian homes, and to have tea at the beautiful home of the Portuguese judge!

What fun Millie and I had sitting on the tall front steps of the Baptist Villa after a long Sunday when we had met with various groups that were speaking English, Chinese, Indonesian or Portuguese! We relaxed as we hashed out our work and our experiences with the various groups. Millie's dear helper would bring us refreshments and tea. One of the treats I enjoyed at Millie's house was when Ah Hang would fix the special Ceylon tea that friends had sent to her.

Millie took missionary, Vi Marie Taylor, to the famous Macau casinos. Vi Marie was quite surprised, and told this story about Millie:

I first saw Millie operating in crowded Macau where she was the only Southern Baptist missionary living on the field, although others lived in Hong Kong and commuted. My first-and-only, inside view of the chief occupation of many people of Macau came when I followed Millie into the depths of the building behind the Jai-Alai courts and the gaming tables at the casinos. She was going there to invite some of the operators of the games to come to Mandarin language Bible study after they got off work.

And they came! Long past midnight, there was a lively discussion going on in Millie's living room, with these young people recently arrived from the mainland, probably taking part in the first free discussion they had ever had.

Cousin, Dick Chauran, decided to have a suit made while he was in Macau because he heard they were well done and often cheap. He was amused when Millie went, too. Dick said,

Mildred went with Pauline and me to this tailor shop that had been recommended to her. The tailor took all my measurements. We looked at materials. The one I liked best he couldn't get because it was only available in

Hong Kong, and a tropical storm made travel on the ocean impossible for a few days. As I was looking over other choices, Mildred asked the man, "Are you using new thread?"

"Yes, I'm using new thread," he replied.

"Let me see it," Millie said.

So he had to bring the thread out and show it to her. When I showed the tailor the new choice of material that I wanted, Mildred asked, "Is that really good material?"

"Yes," he answered.

"Are you sure?" she questioned.

"Yes, I'm sure," he replied.

"Use new thread on it," she insisted.

Evidently, tailors over there have been known to use old thread that in a short time breaks, so that a beautifully made suit is ruined. I've still got my suit. It doesn't fit anymore, but I've still got it.

When my husband's stepmother, Fina Lambert, and her daughter, Jeanette, visited Millie in Macau, Jeanette was fascinated by the Border Gate between China and Macau. It could be seen from one side of Millie's yard. Jeanette wanted to see the area a little closer, but Millie did not encourage her. One day, Millie's young friend - a journeyman missionary, came to visit and meet Millie's company. Both the girl and Jeanette were college age and they "hit it off" right away. The young missionary said she would take Jeanette sightseeing and shopping for a while. They left a little after 10:00 in the morning. In a little while it started to rain, but they did not return for lunch. The rain continued and intensified, but the girls were still not home at suppertime. By this time, both Millie and Fina were becoming very worried - two young girls in a foreign country in the rain after dark! Ah Hang tried to calm Millie and Fina by serving tea and telling them, "Come in, sit down; at the doorway, you will just get wet." They didn't know what to do or whom to call. At about

10:00 at night, the girls showed up in a taxi that had made it up the steep hill in the rain. There was a young man with them who brought them all the way to the house and came in to explain to Millie and Fina that there was nothing wrong. He had been taking care of them to see that no harm came to them. The hard rain made it very difficult to find a taxi, and that was why they were so late. They thanked him, and he soon left.

As soon as he was gone, Fina asked Jeanette, "Where have you girls been?"

"At the Border Gate," she answered. "That is where he works!"

He had shown them all the dorms on the Portuguese Macau side of the border but, of course, could not show them anything on the Chinese side. Millie was amazed they had even gotten near the place, or that any soldier would actually have shown them inside. China kept the gate tightly closed and no one was allowed to enter that country. Indeed, most people were afraid even to get near the area. The girls were too young to realize the potential dangers of where they had been. The Macau rules state, "Visitors may approach within 100 yards of the Barrier Gate, but as it is a military area, photographs are strictly prohibited."

One thing that fascinated Fina, in both Hong Kong and Macau, was men bringing their pets to the park - no, not dogs or cats, but birds! Many men, especially those who were retired, carried a caged bird to a park or square where they put them on a bench or hung them in the trees. The birds were to enjoy the fresh air, and "talk" to the other birds, also mostly in cages.

Fina found another thing a little disconcerting. Just above the mission compound at the top of the hill was an old fort, the Citadel of Sao Paulo Do Monte, which was used to defend Macau against the Dutch in 1622. The fort was now a museum and a weather observatory, but "... a cannon still pointed right at Millie's kitchen window."

"Millie's Life Inspired Me "

Millie was very impressed by a young blind girl, Lucy Chin, from Canton that she met in Macau. She had taught herself Braille and was studying in regular high school classes. She helped Lucy understand geography by making paper mache maps. They became life-long friends. On the Eve of Millie's retirement Lucy gave this tribute:

> Through all these years until now, God has used Millie to open many doors for my growth, development, training and education. I shall never forget when I was a teenager at Sacred Heart School, an English Secondary School in Macau, that I was so desperate to get the geography map explained to me, so I could take my school tests. Millie came to my rescue. From her house helper, I learned that she worked long hours at night in order to put the maps of North America into paper mache relief maps and written words. That certainly was a big job.
>
> I remember the many afternoons when I went to lunch with Millie and her mother at the flat in Macau. Millie introduced me to American silverware which included knife and fork. She showed me how to set the table American style. I can still hear her mother say, "Lucy, I am as proud of you as if you were my child." They were both so good to me and helped me in many ways.
>
> I shall never forget the many weekends AhWor and I spent in Millie's flat in Macau; how we went together to our blind friends' homes to conduct Bible classes with other blind friends. We sat with them in their homes and in the streets. Then we would sit together in her flat sharing with each other our mutual burden and concern for the Lord's work.
>
> We worked together to transcribe the Bible into Cantonese Braille. Millie took all of us blind girls to Caine Road Baptist Church so that I could show them how to use the stylus. Then as some of the girls in the

church read the Bible in Cantonese at dictation speed, they transcribed the words into Cantonese Braille. I helped with the proofreading and Elaine Hancock duplicated copies to be distributed to Braille readers here in Hong Kong, also in Macau, in Malaysia and China. Although this project was later taken over by the Ebenezer School for the blind, I am so thankful for starting this project and the great part Millie had in it. She also encouraged the Board in Blue Mountain to become interested, and they have given their generous support.

It was Millie who put me in touch with Etlan Wilson, her blind classmate at the Southwestern Baptist Seminary, who later offered me a scholarship to study there. Now both he and his wife have remained my great friends. During my last year of studies in the United States, when I was seeking God's will for my life, I saw that the Lord was definitely calling me to return to Hong Kong. God brought to my mind the time when Millie first went to Macau. Although she spoke fluent Mandarin, she took much pain and effort to learn Cantonese so that she could talk with the people. This helped me to realize (since Cantonese is my first language), there is no reason I would not return to Hong Kong to share with the people what I have learned.

In 1978, I started as a Hong Kong government social worker. Later I was transferred from doing exclusively blind welfare work to general rehabilitation with the physically and mentally handicapped and also with the elderly people. God used Millie's love, caring, and concern to open many doors for me.

I have many happy memories, and whenever I think of Millie, I am thankful to the Lord for His calling of her to minister to people in this part of the world as a missionary. Although I must admit I don't easily get inspired, Millie's life has been an inspiration to me. I pray that the Lord will give me the vision, the insight that was given to her, and that I too, like Millie, will be sensitive to the needs of others.

Lucy Chin

Millie continued to be proud of Lucy! She was decorated by
the Queen of England, and later was given a Doctors Degree by
Hong Kong University. Lucy also wrote a book, *One of the Lucky
Ones,* that was the WMU Round Table Group Choice Book for
July 1990!

Clarence

As far back as I can remember, Millie had a red plush, toy
rabbit. Well, not really plush. The fur was mostly rubbed off,
especially on his tummy, which was sort of worn gray cloth. A
battered rabbit he was, but Clarence was also well loved. He went
to college, he went to seminary, he even became a "missionary" to
China. He always lay at the top of Millie's suitcase when she
traveled. At home, he slept on her bed.

In 1949, just before the Communists took over Guilin, Millie
sent a small trunk of her things to me in St. Paul, Minnesota. There
were some Chinese silk wall hangings, a tiger rug, and Clarence on
top. Clarence! I was shocked to see him. I couldn't imagine her
parting with him. I believed that Millie thought she would never
get safely out of China.

She was under the Communist regime for a very tense year and
a half before she was given an exit visa and ordered to leave China.
Even then, she didn't come home to America because she was ill.

When Millie was well enough to travel, she returned to the
United States on furlough and she headed for Minnesota to see me,
Al (my husband), and to pick up Clarence. She left the other
things, and the trunk with me for safekeeping. This turned out to
be a bad decision because I eventually lost them in a move, but at
least Clarence was safely back with Millie, traveling on top of her
clothes in the suitcase. He went to conventions and camps; he

visited coast-to-coast and he made trips around the world. Clarence lived in Hong Kong, and then in Macau. Millie's *amah* used to think it was very silly for a grown woman to keep a toy rabbit, especially one that was so worn and old.

On one furlough in the 70's, Millie came home and visited us in our new home and state - California. When she opened her suitcase to give me a little present, I saw that Clarence was not on top. He didn't seem to be anywhere. "Where is Clarence?" I asked.

"Oh," she said, "I gave him back."

"Gave him back! To who?" was my question. (I know I didn't use correct English, but when you are that astonished, it doesn't matter.)

Then Millie told me that before I was born, she had gotten Clarence from another missionary child in a Canadian family. This family had a daughter just older than Millie whose name was Christine. The mother thought it would be nice for her daughter to share one of her toys with Millie to comfort her on the long journey to the United States. The mother chose Clarence. Millie was reluctant to take him because she felt Christine did not like this arrangement at all. The mother insisted. So Clarence joined Millie's things, and lived and traveled with her for fifty years!

On this particular furlough, as Millie traveled to Toronto to see some friends, she found Christine again. They talked about being children in China and Christine asked Millie if she remembered the red rabbit her mother had forced her to give away.

"Oh yes, Clarence," said Millie. "Do you want him back?"

The amazed Christine screeched, "Do you still have him?"

"Yes," Millie replied. "He's in my suitcase now. I'll get him for you."

So after all his years of travel around the world, old tattered Clarence was returned to his very pleased original owner, and moved to a new home in Canada.

Several people gave Millie little stuffed toys to replace Clarence and she enjoyed all of them, but finally someone came up with the perfect gift - a beautiful, 'Cabbage Patch'-type, Chinese doll who, instead of a birth certificate, had identification papers as a stateless refugee. So many people in Hong Kong and Macau were stateless refugees from China, Indonesia, Burma, Vietnam and many other places. They did not have passports but only identification papers. Millie loved, encouraged, and tried to help these people who had no country to call home. It was very easy for her to love her new beautiful, stateless doll.

The Billy Graham Crusade

Missionaries, Steve Baker and Fay Taylor, were impressed with Millie's persistence when Hong Kong was host to the Billy Graham Crusade in the fall of 1975. Hong Kong is only about forty miles from Macau and there is good transportation by ferry or hydro-foil, but there were many people in Macau who could not go to Hong Kong even though they had the money for the fare. Hong Kong was British and Macau was Portuguese, so it was a matter of going from the territory of one country to another, and they were stateless - refugees from other countries who did not have legal travel documents.

When the crusade was still two months away, Millie thought of some ideas for the people of Macau and she started contacting the people in Hong Kong who were in charge. "No, Billy Graham could not work it in his schedule to come to Macau for even one night." Millie would not give up: "There must be something we can do!"

She rallied the pastors of all the churches of Macau. Finally, after further consultations with Hong Kong, and working with the local church people, a plan was put into motion. Local combined choirs from the churches would sing together, Ted Smith would come to play the piano, George Beverly Shea, with his wonderful, deep voice, would come to sing, and one of Billy Graham's associate evangelists would preach. With Millie's initiative, encouragement and undying spirit, Macau had its own mini-crusade. All went according to the plan. The territory's main auditorium was filled, and many made decisions to receive Christ as Savior. Steve said he saw that night what can be done with the efforts of one committed, determined follower of Jesus Christ!

Fay said,

> The next day there was a businessmen's luncheon featuring George Beverly Shea in testimony and song. It was wonderful! Lady Leandro, the wife of the governor of Macau came. Even the Bishop of Macau was present. After the concert, all were invited for lunch at one of Macau's good hotels. We were told it would be Dutch treat (everyone would pay for their own meal), but when we went up to pay the bill, we were informed that a well-known member of the colony had taken care of it all. He was a famous Chinese developer and gambler, and, as far as Millie knew, he certainly was not a Christian. Amazing!

So Many Refugees

Millie was interested in reaching all groups that were not actively being witnessed to by anyone else. She had so many different projects going on in both Macau and Hong Kong that she often got other missionaries involved too. She sometimes wore them out, as well as herself. Rosie Wong who had immigrated to Hong Kong and Macau from Burma said that Millie reminded her of a certain god in India who had many moving hands and arms. When cousin, Johnny Skoglund, was teaching in Hong Kong, he said a missionary friend remarked, "We all thank God for Millie, but we thank God there is only one Millie!"

Millie was very interested in all people of all races and nationalities. Often she noticed a group of people that others did not see. Fellow missionary, Dick Lusk, wrote,

> One thing I especially remember about Millie was her God-given gift to know and minister to people usually overlooked by the rest of us. Many Portuguese government officials, as well as storekeepers and housewives, were touched and befriended by Millie. She loved young people and those who were blind. Much of her ministry time was given in working with them. Millie was a special ambassador for our Lord Jesus; loved, respected, and admired by those who had the privilege of knowing and working with her. Her love for China and the Chinese people was evident to all.

The Burmese

Most of the people in Macau were Chinese, but there were notable exceptions - the government was Portuguese, and there were many refugees from other parts of Asia and Africa. The refugees often had the poorest jobs and worked the longest hours. Many young people in small factories worked up to twelve hours a day. She noticed that many were Burmese who had quickly left Burma when their government changed. They knew so little Chinese; Millie knew no Burmese, *but* she knew missionaries who did.

Southern Baptists had never been sent to Burma. However, American Baptists had been working there since Adoniram Judson arrived in 1814. Burma was one of their biggest mission fields and always had many missionaries there until they were expelled by the present government.

Two former Burmese missionary couples were just over in Hong Kong, Bill and Marion Hackett and Harold and Estelle Schock. Of course, they were busy with their own mission projects: Bill, Marion, and Estelle taught at colleges and seminaries and Harold worked with drug addicts, teaching them about Jesus who had the power to break their addiction. Yet, maybe they could help her, too. Millie contacted them.

Millie and Burmese young people at the Missionary House

They were happy to work with Burmese people again. Every weekend the Hacketts or the Schocks came to Macau. Usually they took turns, but often both came. Marion Hackett was usually unable to come to Macau because of painful health problems. She needed to save her limited strength for teaching in Hong Kong, but she wholeheartedly supported Bill in the Macau work, and she translated materials into the Burmese language.

During the week, Millie kept in contact with some of the Burmese young people who were learning Cantonese. She couldn't help them much because of their long working hours, but she was thrilled that now they had weekend missionaries of their own. Some were already baptized believers. Soon they had a church of their own. Bill Hackett later recounted in letters that he had actually spent thirteen years of weekends in Macau working with the estimated 25,000 refugees from Burma before he retired in America.

Harold and Estelle Schock were still working with the Burmese when Millie retired. The Burmese Baptist Convention hoped to send their own missionary pastor and wife to the church in Macau, but at the time they were unable to get exit visas from Burma. However, as the Schocks were getting ready to retire, God was preparing another Burmese couple to work with the people, Rev. Philip A. Hone and his wife.

In 1987, on one of Bill's many trips back to Burma, he again visited the church in Macau and was thrilled to see that attendance had gone up 300% and that 35% of those attending had not yet been baptized but intended to be. Bill met with Harold Schock and the new couple who requested the old missionaries lay their hands on the heads of the two of them, and pray that God would especially lead them. This they gladly did.

In many ways, Millie and Bill were alike. They had both been born and grew up on an American Baptist mission field - Millie in China, Bill in Burma. Both became missionaries and returned to serve the country where they had been born. Both countries eventually expelled all their missionaries. Millie and Bill desperately wanted to keep in touch with their homeland friends and help them in any way they could. They wrote many "careful" letters. Both tried to get "home" to their original field of work, often saving most of their money for that purpose. Both worked with young people and often helped pay their way to conferences ... and they both managed to get visas to enter their homeland when others thought it was impossible.

Bill had been able to get a visa into Burma two or three times a year since he had been expelled. Other Burmese missionaries marveled at his persistence. Like Millie, he openly brought in Bibles, hymnbooks, commentaries, and other Christian materials.

Many of the Chinese and Burmese from Macau emigrated to other countries when they were able. Millie tried to keep up with not only the Chinese but also the Burmese, especially if they came to the United States. This was also true of Bill and Marion. Many of the Chinese had been their students in Hong Kong.

Once when Millie was visiting me at Christmas time, a family came over to visit and brought an entire meal in heavy cooking pots. The father and child spoke some English as well as Cantonese. The mother and grandmother spoke only Cantonese. I didn't understand much of what was going on. Before they left, Millie asked what was their emigration status. The father replied in English, "We all have our U.S. citizenship now."

Millie looked doubtful and explained, "But that isn't possible until one knows and speaks English."

The old woman smiled and said, "We speak English now."

And indeed she could - slowly, but correctly. Millie had been speaking to them in Cantonese, so when they all switched to English, I was surprised to learn that they were originally from Burma, and had twice learned to speak a completely   new language. In whatever language, they were grateful for Millie's friendship and concern for them through the years.

The Indonesians

Another group of refugees that Millie became interested in were the Indonesians who had escaped to Macau from the tyranny of President Suharto. A missionary friend, Fay Taylor, had served for quite awhile in Indonesia and was now stationed in Hong Kong. Millie convinced Fay to come over to Macau the first Sunday evening of every month to meet in her home with Indonesian families for worship, Bible Study and fellowship. They started with five families. As the group became much larger, they asked Fay to come twice a month and they had to move from Millie's home to a Chinese Baptist Church.

In 1973 when Fay Taylor left on furlough, retired Indonesian missionaries, Dr. and Mrs. Buford Nichols, came to Macau to lead this Christian fellowship for two years. Then Fay took over again until her retirement in 1982. George Trotter and his wife helped for a while, and so did Millie's friends, Charles and Sara Mullins (although they had to use an interpreter). When Millie retired, the Indonesians had their own building and were organized as the *Hak Sa Wan Baptist Church.*

We, the Lamberts, got acquainted with one of Millie's Indonesian families - Timothy Sie, his wife, and two children. They had escaped from Indonesia and, since they were ethnically Chinese, they emigrated to China. (Talk about "out of the frying pan and into the fire"!) Eventually, they were able to escape out of China to Macau. At last they had freedom, but no chance for good jobs. Both Timothy and his wife were well educated *and* they knew English. I believe they both had Doctors' Degrees. Timothy had a brother in Los Angeles, California, where they hoped to settle. Millie accompanied them to Hong Kong for the interview with the United States Embassy and helped with other problems to prepare them to emigrate. It was over two years before they got visas. During this time, Timothy was baptized at Macau First Baptist Church.

Millie asked my husband, Al, at that time pastor of First Baptist Church in Bellflower, California, if our congregation would help sponsor a displaced Chinese Indonesian family. Yes, we would. Along with Timothy's brother and his wife, we were at the airport to meet the family and welcome them to the United States. The church arranged for a home, food, and furniture. After only four days, Timothy got a job as a chemist in Los Angeles. Timothy said,

> Although my contact with Mildred was for a short time only, this short time was an important time in my life.

Services in Vietnamese, Chinese and English

Dick Chauran said,

> Cousin Millie took us to a youth conference in Macau that was all in Chinese, and later to a church service that

was in Chinese. We couldn't understand a word of it. Even the songs they sang from the songbook were not familiar hymns, although I guess, sometimes they are. Of course, no one called on us to participate.

One evening when Millie was busy elsewhere, Sara Mullins, Pauline and myself went close to the border near the refugee area to the Burmese church. Charles Mullins was officiating at a baptismal service. The lady in charge, Grace Lew, asked Charles if Sara sang. Charles answered, "Both Sara and Pauline Chauran sing." So Sara and Pauline were asked to sing a duet, quite impromptu. They sang "Amazing Grace" because that is what the Chinese girl could play on the piano. Since Charles mostly spoke and knew only English, that *Vietnamese* baptismal service in the *Burmese* church was being translated by Grace Lew into English, Vietnamese and Chinese! It was really interesting. There was even a tea party after the service.

Even in Macau, some people know English better than any other language spoken in the territory, so Millie would bring her Western visitors to the English-speaking church where Charles Mullins was the pastor. One day at the end of the meeting, Charles said, "Brother Dick, will you close the service in prayer?" I looked around and then realized he was talking to me! I went completely blank. I never lead in prayer in public. If he had asked me beforehand, I would have said, "No", but I finally prayed.

Missionaries like Charles and Millie take for granted that any Christian can do everything just as easily as they do. They live the verse - *"I can do all things through Christ who strengthens me"* (Philippians 4:13).

Ah Hang

During her many years of service in Hong Kong and Macau, Millie had two very faithful *amahs* (lady servants). I didn't know the first one, but I certainly got acquainted with her second, Ah

Hang. She was a very humble woman who required very few comforts or possessions. She slept on a board of plywood with only a bamboo mat on it. Her pillow seemed to be a block of wood thinly covered with a layer of cotton and burlap. We figured that only Ah Hang could sleep on that thing.

Millie in front of Mission House in Macau

At times, it was hard to tell who was the *amah* because Ah Hang often managed and bossed Millie. She liked working for Millie because it was easier than the usual place for a woman her age - staying in the home of a son and taking care of the house and children while the daughter-in-law worked.

Ah Hang thought it was very silly for a woman like Millie to keep an old stuffed rabbit toy (Clarence). She decided that it must be because Millie was a single lady, and had no children of her own. She was absolutely baffled when I ... her sister, Edie ... came to Macau with Belinda, my old rag doll, in my suitcase. After all,

I had a husband, four children, and several grandchildren. She thought both Millie and I were slightly deranged as we took pictures of Belinda in a moon festival cart. Later at Christmas, I sent Ah Hang a little furry toy snake. Millie was surprised I knew the New Year was the year of the snake ... I didn't. Ah Hang was actually quite pleased because she was born in the year of the snake. I don't think she kept it long. Things like that would only clutter up her simple life. I believe she gave it to a grandchild.

Like everyone else my daughter, Faith Keller, got a big kick out of Ah Hang. She said,

> Ah Hang was a feisty little woman who took very good care of Aunt Millie's home needs so she could devote most of her time to ministry. She seemed to know all of Millie's family from snapshots and stories she had been told. When we arrived in Macau as newlyweds, Ah Hang felt it to be her duty to fatten up my very lean husband, Phil, in a healthy manner. She cooked large amounts of food and provided extra snacks. The one thing she would not tolerate, though, was Phil's use of two teaspoons of sugar per cup of tea. She heatedly pointed out to Phil that so much sugar was unhealthy as well as costly - all of this through Aunt Millie's interpretation. Phil and Ah Hang continued their interplay over the sugar issue the entire 2+ weeks we spent there. Phil would put one teaspoon of sugar in his cup, wait until the tea was served and Ah Hang had returned to the kitchen, then put another teaspoon of sugar in his teacup. Suddenly we would hear Ah Hang voicing strong Cantonese statements from the kitchen. Aunt Millie would translate, "Ah Hang wants you to know that she knows you have put more sugar in your tea, Phil." I think Ah Hang came to enjoy this act as much as Phil did, although she continued to be stern about it. We met her again, six-and-a-half years later when Aunt Millie brought Ah Hang to the States with her. She again commented to Phil that he needed to gain weight and use less sugar in his tea. She heartily approved of his three little offspring, though.

Missionary, Donna Kirby, admitted,

When I was a fairly new missionary in Hong Kong, Millie was serving as a deaconess at a Hong Kong Baptist Church, the church where I was an active member. One time she invited all the deacons and deaconesses to her home for a meal before she returned to the United States on furlough. Millie, not being a cook, relied on her household helper, Ah Hang, but that time she wanted to cook a more Western meal, so I told her about a chicken and rice dish that I had served to Chinese friends many times. Although it was baked in an oven instead of steamed the Chinese way, I was sure they would like it very much. All she needed to do was put this dish in the oven, have Ah Hang cook some vegetables and have fruit for dessert. The best part, I thought, was that it was so quick and easy that there would be no way that Millie or Ah Hang could fail in preparing it. I told her how, and she and Ah Hang followed the instructions and got it in the oven to bake.

After the cooking time was almost up, Ah Hang thought it was too dry, but Millie would not let her spoil it by adding water even though I had explained that more water could be added. In the end it was rather dry and hard around the edges, but Millie's gracious Chinese friends all said the flavor was very good. Her Chinese friends and co-workers loved her for who she was and for her love for the Chinese people, so the evening was a success in spite of the rice.

After that, I decided not to help Millie cook any more no-fail dishes. It was better to leave it all in the hands of an expert, like Ah Hang.

Missionary, Katheryn White, has this Ah Hang story:

I had made a pecan pie for a gathering of the "singles" with precious pecans sent from the States. Millie couldn't be there, so I saved her a piece. She put it in the refrigerator with the intent of eating it the next day. The next day, she looked for it and not finding it, asked her Amah if she knew about the missing piece of pecan pie.

The Amah admitted that she thought Millie did not want it, and she ate it. Millie expressed a bit of anger toward the Amah, and the Amah quickly reminded her of a recent time when Millie ate the last piece of moon cake that she had been saving. So they both had a good laugh over it. Millie's Amahs were family to her, and she loved each dearly.

Pauline Chauran said:

Dick and I visited cousin Millie in Macau for three weeks. Since we were going to be there for some time, I felt that I should help cook, do dishes, and put things away. Ah Hang didn't agree. She was in charge of the kitchen! We were Millie's guests, and it wasn't fitting for a guest to help around the house. I knew we were making extra work for her; I didn't feel right about having her wait on us for all that time. (I'm not sure that she knew that very few Americans have servants - certainly none of us do.) Finally with Millie's help, she agreed that I could take the dishes off the table, and bring them to her at the kitchen door. She would take them from me there. We were not allowed in her kitchen. I learned to say to Ah Hang, "Hello", "Good morning", and "Thank you" in Chinese.

On a trip in a van in China, we all had to get out and walk on to the ferry that would take us over the Pearl River. All, that is, all except Ah Hang! The driver said, "Grandmother, you can ride on the van." The small ferry only held about six cars, three on each side. We probably could actually see the wide, yellow, dirty-looking river much better outside of the van. When the ferry was safely across to the other side and the van was back on firm ground, the rest of us were allowed to get back in. There was something about Ah Hang that made people respect her.

Pauline's husband Dick related,

Most days cousin, Mildred, took us down into town, but one day she was too busy, so we walked down by ourselves. Ah Hang saw us and was worried that we

might get lost. She sent the mission gardener down to
follow us wherever we went. Of course, he couldn't
speak English to us, but he knew us, and watched over us
as we enjoyed the little shops under the apartment
buildings, the little factories with maybe three or four
workers, the older people visiting and drinking tea or
playing cards. I think Ah Hang was relieved to see us
arrive safely back.

When we were ready to leave, I asked Mildred, "What
would be appropriate for us to get for Ah Hang? We
could go to town and buy something."

"Do you have any American money on you?" she
questioned.

"I have a ten, a five, a couple of ones, and some change,"
I replied.

"Just give that to her," Millie said.

She accepted the money. She probably could have gotten
a very good exchange for Macau money, but she didn't
spend it. She kept it. It was her souvenir.

In 1980, Millie brought Ah Hang with her for a quick
one-month furlough to the United States. Millie especially wanted
to be with our 92-year old father in Oregon. Ah Hang enjoyed this
special trip and was quickly absorbed into the family life of
Millie's relatives and friends. John and Daisy Skoglund visited
Cherry Grove and were amused to see that Ah Hang had taken over
the kitchen at the family home. She prepared lunch for about
fifteen people. Her main dish was fried rice flavored with Kinwah
Ham from Chekiang Province which she had brought from China.
They felt she was truly a remarkable woman.

Niece, Bonnie Evans, was visiting Oregon when Millie and
Ah Hang were there. She said,

Once Ah Hang and I were left alone in Cherry Grove
with sleeping baby, Amy. The house seemed so quiet,
but Ah Hang and I couldn't talk each other's language.
Suddenly, I had an idea. I sat at the piano and started to

play the old hymns. Ah Hang joined me and sang in Chinese as I sang in English, both singing in our native languages our common faith in the Lord.

After I had quit playing, I suddenly saw a huge wasp in the house. It flew into the bathroom, and I quickly shut the door. How could I warn Ah Hang? I took a piece of paper and drew a wasp on it. Then I took the drawing to Ah Hang and pointed to the door. She nodded; she understood. When Aunt Millie returned, she was pleased that we had found ways of communicating.

Millie and Ah Hang brought Papa with them to Southern California for the marriage of our son, Jon Lambert, to Rhonda Fowler. It was strange for Ah Hang to be a guest instead of a servant. It was hard for us English-speaking folks to even tell her how she might help, but she soon figured this out for herself. She picked up and rocked our crying grandbabies, singing to them softly in Chinese. They seemed to understand and were soothed. Every time someone started doing dishes, Ah Hang came into the kitchen and either washed or dried as she shoved the now extra person out. We told Millie, "If we ever have a mob scene like this again, please bring or send Ah Hang. She is very useful."

Ah Hang asked Millie many questions before the ceremony and was very shocked that no one had given Rhonda anything gold to wear. She personally took care of this bad oversight and gave Rhonda a gold bracelet from China to wear during the wedding and to keep forever. (I guess this is for good luck.) Later Rhonda had trouble with the chain breaking because the gold content was so high (18 carats). She had it made into a ring with some American gold (14 carats) added.

Papa, from his wheelchair, had a part in the ceremony. Ah Hang sat beside Millie with the family and later proudly had her picture taken with the bride and groom, and the rest of the Lamberts.

When Ah Hang returned to Macau, she loved to tell about her international travels .... "When I was in Toronto, Canada and visited Niagara Falls .... The gardens in Vancouver, British

Columbia are so beautiful ..., and when I went to a wedding in California, I visited Disneyland."

When Millie retired, she personally set up a small pension for Ah Hang so that she could retire also.

Pictures of Ah Hang in U.S. - Niagara Falls and Disneyland

Riding with Millie

Millie was a good driver - how else could one survive driving in Hong Kong or Macau? But she could get distracted! And, when driving in America she could forget which side of the road we drive on, and which she was supposed to be on, especially after turning a corner. Many people had interesting experiences while driving or riding with Millie. Here are a few of them:

Riding with Millie in England - Missionary Sue Merth

I heard this "Millie Story" from a friend, Evelyn Schwartz. Millie, Evelyn, and a missionary from Korea (either Irene Branum or Ruby Wheat) were all traveling through Europe en route home for a furlough. When they arrived in England, they rented a car with Millie as the driver! (Unbeknownst to them, Millie had just recently gotten her driver's license.) They took off through the English countryside and from all accounts, it was apparent that Millie was a novice driver.

Of course, it wasn't much better when they took a train. Millie got them on one going in the opposite direction to where they should have been headed! I heard from Evelyn that on the same trip, they were simply walking when Millie lost her girdle in Trafalgar Square! She picked it up, put it in her bag and walked on!! Millie didn't let such little things bother her.

Forty years before, Millie showed me Hong Kong in my stopover between ships on my way to Indonesia. I saw more of Hong Kong in that 24 hours than I saw the whole four-and-a-half years I lived there! She was a good tour guide because she wasn't afraid to go any place and meet anyone. She knew Hong Kong. She was such a wonderful Christian and witness for her Lord.

Help on a Ferry Ride - Missionary Ida Lusk

In 1964, the Macau Baptist Church, the mother church of
all Baptist congregations in Macau, had a dedication
service for their new Educational Building. We were
soon to move from Hong Kong to Macau, so I really
wanted to attend this service. However, my husband,
Dick Lusk, was in America, and we had four little girls.
The youngest was less than two months old. Millie knew
how important this was for me, so she offered to go with
me and help with the girls. I got a passport for our new
baby. The boat trip took four hours (this was before the
days of hydro-foils or jet-foils). We made the trip just
fine thanks to Millie's help, good cheer, and laughter.

Driving in Hong Kong- Millie's niece, Faith Keller

In 1974, Phil and I drove with Aunt Millie to the Western
Union building in Hong Kong. She parked in a "No
Parking" zone intending to dash in, take care of her
business, and dash out again. Phil and I waited in the car.
A few moments later, a Hong Kong policeman was
tapping on Phil's window informing him, in no uncertain
terms, that he was to move on. Phil scooted into the
driver's seat. He still quakes when he recalls the trauma
and nerve-racking process of driving in congested Hong
Kong traffic on the wrong side of the road with all of the
controls of the car reversed! On a one-way street, he
went the wrong way for a block. Somehow or other, we
managed to find our way back to Western Union, where
Aunt Millie was waiting on the sidewalk. A shaken Phil
was delighted to give her back the driver's seat.

Riding in Luxury - Missionary Steve Baker

In Macau in the 70's, Millie usually took the bus or
walked, even during the hot, humid, summer season. At
that time, the Macau Baptist Mission had no vehicles,

and only a few homes had air-conditioning. One time we were walking along and still had some way to go when she flagged down a taxi. As we sat down hot and tired, she said, "Ah-h-h, one of the nice things about Macau is air-conditioned taxis." Millie liked the simple things in life.

Yes, Radiators Need Water!- Missionary Vi Marie Taylor

Streets in Macau are steep, stony, and very narrow. I rode beside Millie as she expertly maneuvered a van between the pedestrians and parked vehicles. I was glad that I did not know at first that Millie had only a short time before acquired the van to replace a much smaller Volkswagen. But one day as we set out to the islands which were connected by causeways to the tiny mainland portion, the van stalled on a little village street and started shooting off steam. We discovered that there was no water in the radiator. After making innumerable trips to a water supply at a home by the road, we finally filled it up, and were on our way again. Millie, who had driven only the air-cooled Volkswagen for a long time, exclaimed, "I didn't know you had to put water in a car.'"

Efficiency- Millie's niece, Edie Lovegren

In 1981, I visited Aunt Millie around Christmas time. One day we took a trip to Hong Kong for a whirlwind day of non-stop shopping, visiting friends, and sightseeing. At the very end of the day, we started a headlong rush across town taking various buses to catch the very last hydro-foil of the day which would take us across the bay back to Macau. As we neared the dock, we were caught in a tremendous traffic jam which brought everything to a halt for about twenty minutes. Reaching the next bus stop, we jumped off the bus, ran across a few intersections, ran across the dock, and reached our hydro-foil. Within thirty seconds of us boarding, they lifted the gangplank and we were on our way. I gasped,

"That was close!" to which Aunt Millie replied, "I call that efficient time usage!"

Riding with Millie in Macau- Cousin Pauline Chauran

When Dick and I arrived to visit Millie in 1984, Hong Kong was very hot and steamy even at 5:00 P.M. We quickly took a bus to the ferry docks and soon boarded a wonderfully comfortable hydro-foil for Macau. When we arrived, Millie had me sit in the coolest seat (the front passenger side of the Mission Van that she was driving). Bad idea! With the engine in the back, I felt unprotected. To me everyone was driving on the wrong side of the road and coming right at me. As far as I was concerned, I was sitting in the driver's seat, and I didn't have anything to drive with!

The streets were very narrow and crowded with people. Traffic was horrendous. When Millie wanted to get into a street she honked her horn and then held out her hand with a flat palm signaling the other drivers to stop (a motion one of our policemen might use directing traffic in the United States). It worked in Macau, but she found it didn't work in America.

By the time we reached the Mission House, I had decided from then on to let someone else have the front seat.

What made Pauline's husband, Dick, nervous was the driving in China. He said the bus driver drove on the shoulder and barely stayed out of the way of what seemed like hundreds of bicycles darting in and out. How did they miss each other?

Traveling With Millie in Germany- Cousin June Bruce

In 1970, when I was returning to Kenya and Millie was returning to Hong Kong, we met in Germany to see the Passion Play in Oberamergao. We didn't have tickets, but when we asked at the hotel, they said they could get tickets for us the next day. While waiting, we took a German speaking tour of the beautiful countryside and into Austria. With our background of Swedish and both of us having taken German in school, we were able to get quite a bit of the spiel on the trip, mainly we just enjoyed visiting with each other in such a beautiful setting.

The next day at the Passion Play, we had a book with the script in several languages including English. Sitting next to us was a German couple that had no knowledge of the story of Jesus. They said during intermission they had never heard about it before and were very interested. We gave them our script since we already knew the Bible story. They had never met a missionary before, and were glad to meet Millie. They exchanged addresses. I don't know if they wrote to each other, or if she ever saw them again.

A Short Trip to Washington- Cousin Dick Chauran

A year after Millie retired, she called us and asked if we wanted to go to Hugh and Louise Lovegren's house near the Canadian border. She wanted me, Dick, to help her drive. I said, "All right. Pauline and I will drive up to your house on Friday night and sleep there, and then we can leave for Washington in the morning."

She agreed and thought that would be fine. I hoped I would do most of the driving because Millie would get distracted when there were people to talk to. She would even turn and look backwards to say something to someone in the back seat . I would tell her, "Turn around and watch the road!"

When we started off on Saturday morning, Millie said we had to go by Portland to pick up a girl. It was out of the way, but it seemed the Chinese girl was going with us to visit our cousins. After she was safely aboard, Millie said there was another lady who had been a missionary with her who needed a ride, but just to Seattle. So, we drove to another section of Portland to get the missionary.

Finally we started north to our cousins' house. "Now, Millie," I asked, "did you call Hugh and Louise to tell them we are coming?"

"Oh, yes," she explained. "I told him I was coming."

"Didn't you tell them we were all coming with you?" I asked.

"No," she answered, "but they have plenty of room."

And that is the way it was. There were five coming instead of the one they were expecting. When we did get to the Lovegren's home, Hugh opened the door and said, "Hello, who are all these people?" Pauline had met these cousins years before - I never had and, of course, neither had the Chinese girl from Portland or the missionary. Hugh and Louise were very gracious and found someplace in their home for all of us to sleep overnight.

We left the next afternoon for Seattle where we dropped off the missionary lady. Millie decided we would stay that night with her cousin, Cherry Lois Knight. I asked, "Millie, does she know we are coming?"

"Oh, she has plenty of room," was the answer. I guess Cherry Lois was used to having Millie drop in when she was near Seattle. She did have plenty of room and was glad to meet us.

As we were heading south toward home, Millie remembered that someone was in the hospital in Tacoma that we should stop and see. She might have been a cousin on the other side of the family. We had to turn southwest a ways in order to stop at the hospital. Here were all these people, four of us, who came up to a hospital room to visit a patient, and Millie was the only one she knew.

As long as we were now in Tacoma, Millie said she wanted to go to Seatac Airport because there were some people she wanted to greet who had a stopover between

planes at about that time. We sat at the airport waiting
for about an hour. Finally someone who had been sitting
near us and also waiting a long time walked up to us and
said, "Oh, are you Mildred?"

I guess he had heard us use her name.

"Yes, I'm Mildred," she answered, and they talked for
about two minutes before these folks heard their plane
announced, and they had to board their flight. I don't
know if Millie had ever met them before. I think they
were friends of friends.

Then since we were so close, we went out into the
country to track down someone else that we should "stop
and see".

This trip was actually somewhat typical. This is the way
Millie kept up with "all those people". Everyone was
individually special to her. We expected the unusual
when traveling with Millie.

Lessons in Prayer - Cousin Linda Pearson

In 1990, Lincoln and I sold our home in Portland, and
were delayed getting into our new house in McMinnville.
We stayed with cousin Millie in Cherry Grove for a
couple of weeks until our house was ready. One day
Millie wanted me to go with her into Forest Grove to get
her tires checked. I was glad to do it - I hadn't ridden
with her doing the driving!

Here we were going down this hilly and curvy road with
Millie looking way over to the side. She kept pointing
and telling me about things. She seemed interested in
everything around her except the road. I started quietly
praying hard. It certainly was a fast way to get a person
to pray. God must have heard my prayers because we
got there and back safely. Or, maybe it was Millie's
angels guarding her. Whichever it was - thank you,
Lord!

Millie and Money

Millie had a completely unworldly view of money. If God wanted her to do something, she expected Him to provide the money. She made plans and waited for God to supply her needs. If the money was not forthcoming, she borrowed or made other plans. I remember one furlough when we returned to Cherry Grove, Oregon, after a trip. She had many letters waiting for her. We sat on the bed as she opened each envelope and read page after page. I was amazed that so many contained money or checks. She wasn't surprised.

"Oh, good!" she said, "Now another girl can go to the youth conference."

"Wonderful! I'll use this for Bibles, maybe Braille ones."

"How nice. This should go to Serampore College in India."

Millie helped many young people attend regional, Asian and even international Christian conferences to such distant places as Buenos Aires, Argentina and Portland, Oregon, USA. She worked with the "local" leaders in Korea, Japan, the Philippines, Thailand, Sri Lanka, India, Burma and Singapore. She was especially busy when the young people of Macau hosted the Asian Baptist Youth Fellowship. Through this involvement she became known to a number of Baptist youth leaders in a number of countries, urging them to fellowship with one another, to strengthen their leadership and their resolve to serve Christ. It was a wonderful ministry but it took money, and God usually provided it. She depended on it.

Sometimes this non-worldly attitude got her into uncomfortable situations. Sue Merth remembered an incident years ago when she and Millie were in Chicago for a World Mission Conference. She said, "The weather was very cold as only the 'Windy City' can be in the winter. Millie had come by train or bus and only brought a rather light jacket. When I met her later in the day, she asked if I could cash a check for her. Then she explained why she needed the money. She had arrived in Chicago with only *eighty cents*!

"Millie went on to relate her adventures upon arrival. She wanted to visit one of her many Chinese pastor friends who lived quite a few blocks from the station. Not having money on her for a taxi, she proceeded to walk to his place. En route she became so cold that she stopped off in a little cafe (a truck stop) to warm up a bit. This was not in one of the best parts of Chicago. She was so nonchalant about it all. I would have been terrified."

Dick and Pauline Chauran, cousins of Millie, said that she thought it was a shame that they were just visiting her in Macau when, for only $400 more apiece, they could get plane tickets to visit brother, August, and his wife, Alta Lee, in Jordan in the Near East. Dick explained, "That's $400 more than we have."

She was accustomed to traveling around the world visiting and staying with missionaries and friends along the way. She traveled so much more cheaply than anyone else could, and she wasn't afraid to be stuck anywhere in the world. After all, God knew where she was and how to get her out!

"He knows the way I take" (Job23:10a).

The "Planned" World Trip

When Papa was 90 years old, Millie planned a birthday party for him in *Hong Kong*. My sister-in-law, Viola Lovegren, and I went with Papa on this long journey. It was furlough time for Millie so she planned to return to America with us - *the long way* - around the world. She knew people in so many places that she easily arranged for us to stay with missionary friends or at missionary guest houses. This worked very well in Thailand, and Singapore, but suddenly our travel plans were changed. Monsoon Rains! Calcutta and much of North and East India was flooding.

We were rerouted to Madras in South India. No problem. Millie found an Indian hotel that had corn flakes and boiling milk for breakfast; lunches with *pooree* bread and tea - our tongues and throats couldn't eat any of the hot, spicy sauces that went with it. She introduced us *and herself* to American Baptist Missionaries, Bill and Joyce Scott, who fed us two lovely meals and told us about their work with literacy and Bible distribution (each one, teach one, using Bible lessons as their texts). Impressive!

We got to see the tomb of St. Thomas, the disciple of Jesus who went across Asia and died in India, near Madras. (I hadn't known that!)

Somewhere Millie had met some Telegu Christians from Madras. On Sunday morning, we took a city bus to their church. (Whoops! I learned women stand, unless there is a completely free seat. Never sit down beside a man!) The Christians warmly welcomed us to their services and gave us warm pop after the meetings. Since we were thirsty, it tasted good.

Papa decided he would like to visit Nelore, the heart of the Telegu work, especially the Lone Star Church that he had read about as a young man. A Christian Telegu train official said he would meet us at the depot in the morning and personally put us on the train, a kindness that seemed unnecessary, but proved to be a very wise decision! He got us four seats together in a small compartment with just one other Indian couple and child. People were so crowded on most of the train that people were traveling on top and seated in the windows with their feet hanging in or out. At each stop, vendors sold things through the windows. Millie bought some bananas for our lunch.

I asked Millie, "Who will meet us, and where will we stay?" She didn't think that there was an inn there.

"Don't worry," she said, "you have an American Baptist doctor in Nelore, and we will stay with her."

Sure enough, when we arrived in Nelore, Millie rented five pedicabs (a modern rickshaw with a man on a bicycle providing the power). The extra one was for our luggage. She directed them to take us to the mission hospital. Poor Dr. Marian Boehr was busy with operations. She had a fairly large mission house but little food and nothing prepared for overnight guests.

Millie explained that she was a Southern Baptist missionary in Hong Kong, and this was our 90-year old father, a former missionary to China and Taiwan, and her sister-in-law, Viola, a Southern Baptist from New Orleans and her sister, Edie Lambert from California, an *American Baptist* minister's wife. "Because *she* has heard of your work here, we decided to come and stay with you!" Dr. Boehr had to delay her next operation while she instructed her servant to go and buy food and prepare sleeping places. Then she told her cook what to feed these hungry strangers.

Arriving at the Baptist Hospital in Nelore, India by Pedicab

Nelore, India - Nursing Director, Edie and Dr. Boehr

We had a wonderful, informative, fascinating time. We stayed three days with her, disrupting the schedules of the Telegu dean of the School of Nursing, the school administrators of both the boys' and the girls' schools, the pastor, and, of course, Dr. Marian Boehr and the Swedish nurse, Dorothy Johnson, who assisted her. What unbelievably gracious Christian people!

There were times when Viola and I felt this "missionary tour" took more faith than we had.   Millie and Papa seemed self-confident; we sometimes felt helpless. One night while Viola was awake, she told the Lord, "I am too old for this kind of trip." God's reply to her was, "Abraham was 75 years old when I called him to leave his home for parts unknown. Every place you go, pray for the people." "Okay, I submit", she answered, and she prayed for them the best she could. We found that people in the next two countries desperately needed prayer.

From Madras, we were now routed to New Delhi, the capital of India, and then to Kabul, Afganistan. How exciting; how exotic! Only, of course, we didn't have visas, and Millie didn't know anyone there - yet. She had heard of an eye hospital in Kabul that had several European Christian doctors and nurses, so she decided we would just go to the hospital and see if they had accommodations for foreigners or could suggest where we could stay. She somehow got us visas.

However, at the New Delhi airport, Millie met an Indian woman who suggested a hostel owned by a German lady who was married to an Afghan man. The Indian lady had once stayed there. Our plane got into Kabul just before sunset. What a strange, interesting country! Millie got a taxi and gave him the hostel address, but the driver tried to dissuade her, saying that we would be much more comfortable at the hotel for foreign dignitaries. Millie was insistent - we really didn't have the money to stay at a top price hotel. To our amazement, the hostel turned out to be a good choice. The owner was a very kind *Christian*, and she did have two rooms - a little one for Papa, and a basement room with three beds and a bath for the girls. She also served European-style food for which my stomach was grateful.

We did visit the Noor Eye Hospital and met some wonderful Christian European doctors and nurses who were only able to witness with their lives, their medical skills, and their smiles in this Muslim land. There were no churches here!

On Friday, the Muslim Holy Day, nothing was open except the mosques. Viola and I walked to the small deserted downtown area. We were very surprised to see pink mini-skirts and tops in some of the little shops. All of the women we saw were completely covered in black, including a black mesh veil over their eyes. "Well," Millie explained, "their husbands like to see them dress differently in the safety of their own homes!" Really, that differently?

We were in Afghanistan during a little window of peace. There had been fighting before we came. Kabul continues today to be a bombed, war-torn city. We wonder about and pray for the German woman and her Afghan family, and for those at the Noor Eye Hospital.

Our original plans were to go by Pakistan and then on to Jordan where my brother, August, and his wife, Alta Lee, served as missionaries. Now that was impossible, and we were re-routed to Iran. Both Papa and Millie were pleased. They had missionary friends there, and many happy memories. We were to stay a part of three days and two nights. Good! *No, Not good!* We had not been keeping up with world news as we traveled about, and we were completely unprepared for the hatred and hostile disrespect that was prevalent everywhere. At the airport, we were not given visas, and we did not have our passports stamped that we were in Iran. We were lucky that they did not confiscate them. They were not only unhelpful, but downright rude; they didn't care if we had to spend day and night sitting in the airport until we could fly out in three days.

Millie could not get the phone numbers of her missionary friends from information. She felt if we got near the church, she could find one of their homes. We tried to get a taxi. There were plenty of them, but we didn't want to go with any of the drivers who were pulling and pushing us, trying to get us into their cabs. Millie rescued a lovely, young, Italian college student who was very frightened. She was trying to visit Iranian college friends during spring break.

We finally found a taxi driver who seemed more calm and sensible, and we all - Papa, Millie, Viola, the Italian girl, and I (Edie) got into the cab with all our luggage. As we drove away from the airport, Millie explained that we wanted first to drop off the Italian girl at one address and then to go to the little Baptist church and find a house near it. He drove to the area of the Baptist church and informed us that he would drop us off first and then take the girl where she wanted to go. He absolutely refused to take her first. By now, we were all concerned for her safety. Finally Millie just asked him to let us all out where we were. He agreed but quoted an extremely large sum for our passage, almost all the money we had for our trip! Since our Italian girl knew a little of the Farsi language, she read the small sum on the meter to the driver. This made him very angry.

Millie finally asked him to take us to the American Embassy, and we would pay what they thought was reasonable. Luckily, he reluctantly did that. Yet even at the Embassy, he argued with the official and wanted to keep the Italian girl. He said we must pay not only for our passage, but also for each piece of luggage - each suitcase, purse, camera, etc. It took an Iranian man, who worked at the Embassy, to finally get a price that was high but more reasonable.

The Italian girl was allowed to stay with us. From the American Embassy, she called her friends who soon came to pick her up. They were so thankful that she was safe. Girls traveling alone could disappear.

Even at the Embassy, things were hectic, almost out of control. Secretaries told Millie that her friends had either left or had not registered. The Iranian man seemed to be the only one who cared about us. He felt Papa was not being treated with the respect that age demanded. He wished he could take us home, but he explained he had a very small house and eight children. Since no one at the Embassy wanted us there, the Iranian man got us a taxi driver whom he trusted, and the fare was agreed upon before we got in. He took us back to the turbulent airport.

Millie had looked at the phone number of the Turlingers in the Embassy files and memorized it. At the airport, she called them. They came immediately and got us. They were really disgusted at the non-information we had gotten at the Embassy. They had just registered again that month, and so had the Kirkendahls, Millie's other missionary friends.

As we drove up to their house, Mr. Turlinger pointed to a very nice, large house across the street that had guards around it. He said an important general lived there, and the guards, both night and day, made them feel safer. How glad we were to be in a peaceful place with Christian friends - a place to wash, to lay down, and to sleep. We stayed with them until time to board our flight.

Just a few weeks later, the government of Iran was overthrown by the radical Muslims. The angry people killed the generals, including the one across the street from the Turlingers, and the American Embassy was breached with several hostages taken. The Turlingers and Kirkendahls were able to leave safely. I don't know what happened to the nice Iranian man at the Embassy. I feared for him and his large family.

What a relief it was to finally leave Iran and to arrive in Jordan and be met by our brother, August, and his wife, Alta Lee! Viola and I agreed that we don't appreciate what our missionaries go through to spread the Gospel of Jesus Christ.

Viola said when she got back to New Orleans, "Home never looked sweeter, or freer, or safer!!! I can see why people want to kiss the ground." What a blessing to live in America!

Beautiful Coloane Island

By 1978, there were so many missionaries moving to Macau that the Southern Baptist Mission built an apartment house on the lower compound area where an orchard had been. Millie and Ah Hang were to have a small apartment on the ground floor. While waiting, Millie found a little narrow house in a Chinese fishing village on the island of Coloane. It was about fifteen feet wide with several small rooms one after the other. There was electricity and a bathroom, and Millie did insist on two other "modern" conveniences - a refrigerator and a screen door.

The houses were very close together, the street in front was very narrow, and the people were very curious but friendly. Ah Hang loved it. She ruled the house and managed Millie; she also had taken over the street. When she walked up and down, it was like a mayor on inspection. There were always plenty of people to talk to because the village store was across the street. Millie was busy with so many projects that she didn't get to talk to the

villagers about Christ as much as she wished, but Ah Hang did.
They decided to stay.

When Ah Hang was visiting her son and his family, neighbors
were afraid Millie wouldn't cook rice just for herself so two village
families invited her in for meals or brought food to her door. She
said, "They are so poor, but they share so lovingly of what they
have, and I feel very grateful to them. Coloane is a homey place."

Some younger missionaries worried about Millie living alone
with just Chinese; the older ones explained that for a long time
during the Cultural Revolution, she was the only Southern Baptist
missionary in all of Macau. The Chinese were her people.

Millie had fewer overnight guests on Coloane - they preferred
to stay at the compound apartment building or in the lovely new
beach hotel on the other side of the island. Cousins Johnny and
Daisy Skoglund were the exception.

During one of their college holiday times, Millie asked them to
come to Macau to help her with a young people's camp. They
went. The day before the camp began, Millie tripped over a root at
the campground. She was obviously hurt. They drove her to the
doctor and found she had broken her arm. So, Johnny and his wife,
Daisy, their two daughters, and a granddaughter took over the
camp. At night, Johnny and Daisy stayed at Millie's little house
while the younger family members stayed in tents with the other
campers. Since the young people had never been to camp before,
part of the time it was chaos. One night a cloudburst hit Macau,
causing streams to flow through the tents. The next day there was
sunshine and everyone and everything dried out. The young
people seemed to have a grand time - they said so again and again.
Amazing!

Even when she had to give up her home because of furlough
time, when she came back to Macau, she and Ah Hang would
return to the village to visit. One Christmas she brought three
young people from Pui Ching Middle School to put on a puppet
show on the street in front of her old house. It was called *The Real
Meaning of Christmas*. Both children and adults attended.

Afterward the children went caroling throughout the village and passed out Christmas tracts from the Bible Society.

There was a little Catholic church on Coloane - the Chapel of St. Francis Xavier. Millie liked the priest but worried about where his emphasis was. You see, when the magnificent Cathedral of St. Paul's caught fire during the disastrous typhoon of 1835, only one wall was left standing. The fire was actually a blessing to the people of Macau. The church was on a high hill and on that dark, stormy night, they could see the flames and run from the ferocious flooding waves to safety near the church. Someone was able to save the bones of the Japanese Christian martyrs and a saint that had been relics of St. Paul's. They were brought to the little chapel on Coloane and were kept in two long boxes under the altar. The priest could get so excited showing folks "the bones" that he forgot to tell people about Jesus Christ.

Millie herself had a very sharp and curious mind. She loved to learn about historical things, especially Christian history. The priest's total absorption in the bones helped remind Millie not to let unimportant things become her message.

"For I am determined to know nothing among you except Jesus Christ and Him crucified" (I Corinthians 2:2).

A Youth Camp In Macau

In 1982, Millie invited family members and missionary friends to join her in a tour of West China, including our home town of Losan. My brother, Norman, his wife, Viola, and several cousins and friends traveled to Hong Kong to take her tour.

Viola and I had already discovered that a Millie tour, unlike most travel agency trips, could have some amazing detours. This was no exception. She scheduled the family members to arrive four days early in Hong Kong so that we could see Macau and her work there and rest, recover from jet lag, and so ... surprise! ... *we could help her with a youth camp.* Millie could see so many needs which, in faith, she tried to meet, that it did not usually occur to her that her family might be reluctant to stretch themselves so far in untried ways in a foreign land. She expalined, "It's going to be easy. The young people are children of Portuguese government workers and English children from British business families. There will be no language problems, because they are all at least bilingual. And there are only fifteen of them." Oh, my!

We stayed in a lovely new motel on the island of Coloane. Millie had worked with the Portuguese government to use a park on the island for her camp, where there were even bathrooms and running water. Norman and the other men were assigned to put up the heavy canvas tents. Viola and the women cousins were given tasks like crafts, Bible lessons and cooking meals over an open bonfire.

Millie especially assigned me two jobs that at least were in my strengths ... teaching swimming skills, and leading singing with a guitar. On the mornings, she had arranged to use the swimming pool at the motel where we were staying. The pool was clean. The young people all knew how to swim with varying degrees of skill. Each morning, the pool swimming hour was a pleasure.

The afternoon swim for an hour and a half on a beach in the South China Sea, very near the mouth of the mighty Pearl River coming out of China, was frightening! There were swirling undertows. The water was brownish and of dubious purity. Were those pieces of T.P. floating in that wave?

I asked all the cousins who could swim at all, and who didn't have a pressing task that they had been given to do, to please help lifeguard. I also asked all the young people to be cautious, stay in just one area and close to shore. They cooperated. There would be no teaching of swimming skills in that ocean! I prayed hard for safety *in* the water, and about protection against diseases and infections *from* the water. God was gracious. We all survived.

It really was a beautiful, quiet island. I took the young people on a hike following a stream up into the hills. Such a peaceful place - the green hills, the clear stream, the river, and the South China Sea. Gorgeous!

The music part was a lot easier. Millie said I didn't need to worry about what songs they might know, just teach them songs and hymns I liked. Okay. She gave me a guitar she had borrowed from one of the missionary children in Hong Kong.

"Millie," I said, "two of these pegs won't move. I can't tune these strings."

"Oh," she replied, "the boy told me that but I explained you would find a way."

How? Brother Norman and I finally discovered by tuning the pegs we could move, and putting different sizes of twigs under the frets of the immovable ones that we could almost get it in tune. I didn't strum the bottom string too often. Hopefully the singing drowned out most of the guitar sound.

The first night Millie hadn't had time to get any meat, and it was already supper time. She asked me to go shopping with her. We drove to a house and picked out three chickens.

"I'd like the one under the tree, the one walking by the house, and the brown one hopping by the corner of the fence," Millie said. We waited until the chickens were caught, killed, and plucked. Supper was very late. The hapless chickens, cooked over the open fire were burned on the outside and undercooked on the inside. Luckily the next night Millie bought Chinese fast food for us all.

Everything seemed to take much longer than expected our last morning. By the time we had eaten breakfast cleaned up the dishes and packed our own belongings, it was time to go. We had to get the young people back home, catch the ferry to Hong Kong, and meet the rest of our tour group at the airport. We had to just leave the tents set up, and the camping supplies unpacked. Millie wasn't worried; she said she would just call some missionary in Hong Kong from the airport and tell them to go to Macau and clean up everything ... and so she did. I don't know who the poor missionary was who had to spend his day traveling to Coloane and cleaning up our mess. Whoever you are - thank you!

How did the young people react to our poor efforts? They had all been raised in a gentle Chinese culture. They didn't even seem to know a discouraging, impatient, unhappy English word.

"How delightful," they remarked. "How lovely." "How interesting." "Thank you so very much." They were glad that Millie cared enough to have a camp especially for them. And how did we, tired, jet-lagged, reluctant, foreigners feel after participating in this unexpected and unprepared camp? **Blessed!**

Chapter Six

THE OPENING OF CHINA

After President Nixon's journey to China, things slowly began to change. The Bamboo Curtain became less formidable, and soon limited travel was allowed. A few churches were opened, and then more were renovated and allowed to start services.

If any period of Millie's life could be mentioned along with the verse in the Book of Esther, "And who knows whether you have not come to the kingdom for such a time as this" (Esther 4:14b), the opening of China was that period for her. She was in the right place at the right time. She knew Mandarin, the official language of China, and Cantonese, the spoken language of much of South China. So many of the missionaries who had served in China were gone or now retired. The young missionaries, Millie's age, had been studying Chinese while she had been able to go right to her field, and they had little or no actual missionary ministry in China.

Because we were born in China, Millie knew many of the older missionaries who had served near our parents, and she had kept up with them by letter, and by visiting them when she was home on furlough. Many of these missionaries gave her names of people to greet if she got to their town. Some missionaries were able to take tours with Millie and personally greet their friends. She arranged the tour to include their place of service.

One older, nearly blind missionary said, "When you get to Yaan, just go down the street and tell everyone, 'Emma Brodbeck still loves you!'"

Millie had been carefully writing, not only her old students and fellow workers in Guilin, but also friends of Elizabeth Ward, and families of students or friends in Hong Kong and Macau. She seemed to know people in every province of China.

During the last few years of service in Hong Kong and Macau, Millie was actually assigned to spend one third of her time on Mainland China by either writing or going in on trips. This she gladly did. She also continued to go to China many times after she retired.

A Biting Monkey

Early in 1979 when it became possible, Shirley Smith, Irene Branum, and Millie went to Guilin, China, where both Millie and Irene had served as missionaries, Millie as a youth worker, Irene as a nurse. Before the trip, Millie had especially asked God to help them find some of their old Chinese friends and to be able to be a blessing to them. This prayer was a fairly easy one to answer since they were going to be in Guilin on a Sunday, and the church was already an open one.

It was wonderful for them to be back in Guilin. On the way to church, they walked in a city park, enjoying the lovely lily ponds. Suddenly, three monkeys appeared! They seemed to be a father, a mother, and a youngster. Without warning the father monkey jumped on Millie's back. His arms were over her shoulders and his body reached to her hips. He was big.

The mother monkey became quite upset. Was she jealous? She threw her baby down and rushed toward Millie, grabbing the calf of her leg in a strong and bloody bite. Millie was utterly surprised! She swung her shoulder bag at both monkeys, actually hitting the mother. The father either fell or jumped off her back. All three monkeys ran away.

It had all happened so fast, and in a crowded *city* park, that neither of Millie's friends had a chance to help her. They looked in their purses for something to disinfect the wound. Finally one found a small bottle of perfume. Perfume? Sure. These two nurses knew it had alcohol in it. In a few minutes, they had Millie's wound clean, bandaged, and sweet-smelling. The three of them continued on their walk to church.

How wonderful it was to see the church opened again; how wonderful to see their friends and co-workers; and how wonderful to worship in China again. After the service, the missionary nurses told some of the Chinese about the monkeys' strange behavior and attack on Millie. They were concerned. They insisted that Millie go to the hospital and have the wound checked. In fact, the Chinese went with Millie to be sure she got the proper attention.

Millie was really quite pleased. The hospital was formerly the Zion Baptist Hospital where Irene had worked as a nurse. It was also right across the street from the house where Millie had lived. She was given an injection against infections by one of the doctors. She asked him about any chances that the monkeys might have rabies.

"Oh no," the doctor answered. "None of our local animals are rabid."

Both Millie and Irene got to meet some special friends who were working at the hospital, and hadn't been able to attend church. Not one of them knew that Millie and Irene were in China, much less right in Guilin. How pleased these Chinese friends were to get re-acquainted with their former missionaries. The next day Irene, Shirley, and Millie were welcomed into their homes to meet new family members.

When Millie got back to Hong Kong, she checked with her own doctor. The wound was healing nicely, but her doctor did advise her to take the rabies vaccine, just in case ... fortunately, he had the new vaccine that was given in the arm instead of the older treatment of twelve painful shots into the abdomen. Millie did not have any bad reaction to the monkey bite. Instead she counted it a blessing because in this way they had found some of their precious old friends at the hospital. *Prayers are sometimes answered in very strange ways!*

Forgiveness

The actual service at the Guilin Church was very special to Millie, not only to see her friends, and worship in the newly-opened church, but also to feel a small rebirth of freedoms.

When the Communist troops took over beautiful Guilin, most of the people were thrown into confusion. Suddenly the government controlled their lives. The local citizens were encouraged to give derogatory reports about each other. Missionaries were suspected, Bibles were confiscated, sermons were monitored, and sometimes had to be approved by the government to be sure they were pro-Communist. During church meetings, most pastors had many hymns sung, and a very long Bible reading, and then ended the services saying, "This is the approved sermon" - which they tried to keep very short. It was a tense time for Christians. Well, actually, for everyone!

Through the years, Millie tried to remember to pray for the Christians in China that she knew. She and I often talked about how long-lived the old Chinese missionaries seemed to be. Many in their 90's were still praying for their friends in China. Our father was 95 when he died. Viola Hill was 102 years old when God called her home. So many Chinese pastors and leaders were jailed. Chinese Christians needed all their prayers.

During the early Communist years, one of the frightened young men in the Guilin church reported something against a beloved, saintly, Baptist Seminary professor. The Professor was taken to jail, and he died there. The Christians felt that the reporting young man was a traitor, and they shunned him. He started catching every disease that came around, often becoming very ill as well as despondent.

In the late 70's the government allowed a few churches to be reopened. There was a slight catch to it. Someone in the community had to go to the authorities, declare himself to be a Christian and promise to get two other "ministers" to work with him in opening and establishing a church. The ministers did not have to be seminary trained. A deacon, a Bible woman, any brave Christian leader would do, as long as they were willing to sign. It was hard to find anyone to sign since so many pastors and Christian leaders had been imprisoned and died. Some were now freed but were in poor health, or very old, or both. No longer could churches belong to a denomination, now all Protestant pastors had to work together.

As soon as the sickly "traitor" heard there was a way to open a church, he very bravely went to the authorities in Guilin, signed his name as a Christian, and asked that the church be reopened. Most of his fellow Baptist Christians did not trust him. They felt he was probably a government plant to spy on them. None signed. He was finally able to persuade a Bible lady from "The Little Flock" group. However, she made it plain that if the church should open, she would only attend on the Sundays she was to lead the meeting. Members of "The Little Flock" congregations do not normally attend church with other Christians.

Finally our "traitor", who continued to improve physically, convinced (or more likely, God convinced) another Christian to join him and to sign. Now with three leaders, the church could open. Guilin was one of the very earliest cities to have a re-opened church. Even though people were afraid, they were so hungry to hear God's word and to worship Him that they came.

How wonderful it was when Millie was able to visit China and worship with them. In the summer of 1982, I was delighted to be a part of a Sunday morning service. Millie kept passing notes telling something of what was being said in Chinese, and I recognized the music of the hymns enough to sing along quietly in English. The "traitor" was one of the leaders in the service. The "obstinate" Little Flock Bible woman was coming every Sunday and encouraging her members to do so, too.

That afternoon Millie took me to the apartment of the old Seminary Professor's wife, her son, daughter-in-law and their teenage daughter. They did not attend the open church, but instead had a small group of Christians meeting in their home. The old mother wanted to attend church openly and worship with her many old friends, but Millie told me later that it was too hard for the son to forgive the "traitor" for probably causing his father's death. He couldn't worship where the "traitor" was one of the leaders. Millie seemed to be able to always be friends with people even when they differed drastically. She prayed for both men.

Two years later, when Millie was showing me some pictures of her latest trip to Guilin, I saw that she had taken some snapshots inside the church.

"Millie," I asked, "isn't that the Seminary Professor's son, up there behind the pulpit?"

"Yes," she answered, "he was leading the singing."

"What happened?" I wondered.

Millie explained that God had now given him the grace to forgive the "traitor". Both men were on the platform that morning, working together to serve their Lord. And the professor's old wife was rejoicing in openly worshipping God with dear old Christian friends.

"Our Father in Heaven, forgive us our sins, as we also have forgiven those who sin against us" (Matthew 6:9-12).

The East Mountain Church

Canton is very close to Hong Kong. As soon as Millie began to be able to cross the border, she started making visits to Canton. Here is her report of her early visit during Christmas of 1980:

During each summer I was in Guilin, I would come with others for our annual South China Mission Meeting in Canton and a couple weeks of holiday. Sundays I would attend the dynamic worship services in the nearby East Mountain Baptist Church. The singing of many students from the Pui Ching and Pooi High Schools seemed to lift

lift the roof off. The messages of Pastor Matthew Tong were equally inspiring. One special Gospel chorus I learned in those services stayed in my heart and mind the next thirty years - "Joy Filled My Heart". I dreamed of a day, as God willed, when I would again hear it sung in the East Mountain Church.

As a gesture of openness for a watching world, the Chinese government decided in 1979 to let a few churches in a few large cities in China be re-opened for worship services. A great deal of cleaning and redecorating would need to be done first. The East Mountain Church in Canton (now called Guangzhou) was chosen as the first open church in South China. An interdenominational service was held the first Sunday of September, 1979, and among the pastors leading the service was Pastor Matthew Tong who by God's grace had survived through the years, though enduring much suffering.

As Christmas of 1980 approached, my fellow teachers in the Pui Ching High School Branch in Macau invited me to join them in vans driving up to Canton. They wanted to celebrate the 90th anniversary of the main school in China. I felt honored to be included and asked a fellow missionary, Dr. Vi Marie Taylor, to join us. There were hundreds of alumni gathered on the campus to honor the occasion. Vi Marie and I were the only "big-nosed" (Caucasian) people present, but we were made very welcome.

I was delighted to see in the crowd Pastor Matthew Tong, who came up to us and remarked, "Today you will hear me preach!" The service began at noon. We found a church packed to the rafters with happy people of all ages. Seats had been saved for us. On the side front was a beautiful Christmas tree decorated with homemade greeting cards.

There were fifty robed choir members, and they sang for us a wonderful special rendition of "Silent Night, Holy Night". Then Pastor Tong preached from Matthew 1:23 - "Immanuel, which is translated - God with us." "All

through these past years - God with us!" It was so
moving! So thrilling!

After the service, I talked to several choir members about
my dream of hearing "Joy Fills My Heart" again sung in
this church. They no longer knew it. The pianist asked if
I had a copy, and I brought a copy out of my purse. She
played it, and promised that the choir would learn to sing
it.

Pastor and Mrs. Tong invited me to their home the next
morning. They shared with me their joy in again being a
part of a renewed witness for Christ after many silent
years. Pastor Tong said that they had a Christmas gift for
me. It was a copy of the Chinese New Testament which
had just been printed in Shanghai in *1980* - the first
reprinting of the Bible in Mainland China since 1950.

Bible plates from 1919 had been found stored under old
newspapers in the basement of the Baptist True Light Building in
Shanghai. 50,000 copies were made in that first printing. Millie
said, "From that time until June 1994, the Amity Press in Nanjing
printed a total of *ten million* Bibles and Scripture portions **in**
Chinese, **by** Chinese, **for** Chinese, but that first New Testament is
one of my precious possessions to this day."

Needing A Friend

By the next fall (in 1981), Dr. Vi Marie Taylor, who had
accompanied Millie to the East Mountain Church, was one of the
earliest foreigners invited to teach in Canton, China. She had a
Ph.D. in Education and Administration. She taught a special
seminar to English teachers on how to better teach the English
language, and she also gave a crash course in English to oil
engineers being sent to America for further training. She got along
well, but she was lonely. This is how she explains it:

When I first went to China to teach, I was completely on
my own - living in an overseas Chinese hotel where no
one spoke English. I was using my limited Cantonese to

order my food generically- "ha" (shrimp) might bring
sweet and sour or any number of combinations. I had no
chance to react with anyone to all the new things I was
seeing. But as soon as my address got back to Millie, a
Chinese woman, Sharon, arrived at my hotel room.
Millie had written her where I was and Sharon, who was
raised by a missionary and spoke welcoming, and
welcome, English, had not even put down the letter
before she came to rescue me. We had a good time. She
made arrangements for me to visit her school and talk to
the English teachers there. At Christmas time, when I
had seen only one other American in the interim, Millie
appeared to spend Christmas with me and to attend the
91st Pui Ching School reunion.

Sharon, the Chinese woman, had been one of Millie's student
friends years before in Guilin.

Millie and Sharon, one of her "students" (1949)

The Government and the Chinese Churches

How did Millie feel when the Chinese government started restoring and returning the churches to the people? Millie was thrilled! Yes, the government was still Communist and had strict rules, but she had very little trouble accepting most of the ideas of the Three Self Movement which was the Christian group that the government worked with. The three selves stand for:

1. Self-Government - this meant that no religious group in England, the United States, Italy, or anywhere else could or should control the Christian Church in China. Actually only Christ should be the head of the church. Protestants, who are normally more independent, didn't have as many problems with that as Catholics did, who could certainly still listen to the Pope, but were not to be bound by his decisions. They were to determine for themselves God's will for China.

2. Self-Support - Often times money is used for control or for power ("If you don't do as we say, you won't receive any more mission funding!") The Chinese now wanted to pay their own way in China so that outside forces could not control them. Missionaries didn't mean to control the churches, but many who really weren't considering differences in needs and cultures felt the Chinese churches should be exactly like the ones at home in Canada or the United States, or in Germany - with the same order of service, same hymns, same governing boards, etc.

3. Self-Propagation - If Christianity is really going to be a religion or faith of the Chinese people, then Chinese should be the ones to win Chinese to the Lord. No longer would missionaries from overseas be expected to be the soulwinners of Chinese in China. Missionaries should only come at the invitation, and under the direction of the Chinese pastors.

I think if we were talking about our own churches in the United States, most of us would agree with these Three Self Principles. We expect the Holy Spirit to guide us, to help us win others, and to open the hearts of people to give to their churches. We don't feel the need of some foreign person to explain what should be done in America.

Churches were to respect the government - to cherish a love for their motherland and for their religious faith. We expect our churches to do the same. Many of our congregations even display the American flag with the Christian flag in our sanctuaries. In the Bible, we are admonished to obey our national leaders and pray for them.

The new government rules for Christianity were that a church was either Protestant or Catholic, with no other divisions. Bibles were to be the only Christian text and guide for sermons. Each minister was to preach what he personally felt, and not try to fit in with other's beliefs, Christian believers could choose either sprinkling or immersion baptism.

Some considered this new stance on religion as a blessed miracle, others felt it was a trap for more persecution. Many Americans did not like the elimination of denominations. They felt Chinese should still be Baptist, Anglican, Methodist, Lutheran, Pentecostal, etc., and they felt things would go better if missionaries were still in charge.

Millie had for several years been claiming the verse in Isaiah 43:19, *"Behold, I am doing a new thing; now it springs forth, do you not perceive it?"* For her, this was God's miraculous new thing, that the very government that had closed the churches and tortured the pastors, now opened and renovated the churches, and paid the pastors to preach the Bible. She encouraged Christians to come out of hiding and worship openly, accepting God's splendid new thing. Within a few years, the churches became self-supporting and they now pay their pastors from their own offerings.

The Nestorian Monument

Many times when Millie tried to tell people about Jesus in China and Hong Kong, they would turn aside and say they didn't want to hear about a new Western religion. She would explain that Christianity was the true faith and very old. In fact, it was preached in China before the first white people ever came to America. Yes, this is very true!

Actually, there are some ancient traditions that say in the first century, the disciple Thomas traveled as far as South China. We know he preached in India and is buried near Madras. Millie decided to learn all she could about Chinese Christian history, and especially about old Nestorian Christians. She found many old documents and books that she studied and copied.

When cousins, John and Daisy Skoglund, were living in Bangalore, India, and teaching at Serampore College, Millie came to visit them. She said she believed there was still a Nestorian Church in India, and she hoped to talk to someone about it. John told her, "You have come to the right place. Mar Aprem, the Metropolitan Head of the Church of the East (Nestorian) is a doctoral student in our school. It will be easy to arrange a meeting with him." John and Daisy were able to work it out so that Millie had a marvelous visit with Mar Aprem. He confirmed many of the things she had been learning.

The oldest actual contact between Christians and the Chinese that can be definitely proved was made by Nestorian traveling salesmen. They left behind a monument in Sian. The Nestorian Christian movement was started by Nestorias, an early church leader in 350 to 400 A.D. He lived in Syria with a lot of followers who were dedicated to telling the message about Jesus. Many of his followers were tradesmen. When they traveled as far as the East coast of China, through Central Asia, and up through Russia, they witnessed for Christ. As people came to believe in Jesus, the tradesmen sent back to Syria for a farmer/priest - a monk, who could farm to make a living and teach new Christians to grow crops for their sustenance as he taught them about God and the Scriptures. Thus, a Christian community would be established with a Christian lifestyle. By 800 A.D., there were 900 Syrian Christian churches in China! Some scholars have discredited this great Christian movement saying both tradesmen and monks were not well educated (but then neither were Peter, James, and John and most of Jesus' first disciples).

How did this strong Christian movement disappear? Vicious Chinese warlords conquered, persecuted and killed Christians. Thousands of them! Later the Muslim armies murdered whole Christian communities. Many weak Christian communities in the West apparently felt it was easier to convert to the Muslim faith than to go back to their idols. According to the Koran, they could at least acknowledge Christ as a great prophet and teacher, if not as the Savior. At least it saved their earthly lives. Only God can judge about their souls.

Before 1400, there was a man who was digging a well in his ground when he came upon a large stone. It was made of special granite and had three kinds of writing - formal Syriac, and formal and informal Chinese. One of the people he called over to look at his stone was a Catholic missionary from Italy who was able to read the Syriac. It listed the "People of the Light" and the Christian symbol that the Nestorians used, listing many missionary names. The stone also told basic tenets of our Christian faith - Christ's birth, details of His ministry, and then much more obscurely, the message of the cross.

The stone is in Sian today. Communist tour guides talk about the importance of this old stone, and explain that this is the evidence that Christianity in China dates back at least to 600 A.D. The stone is ten feet high, four feet wide, and eight to ten inches thick. Millie got a rubbing of it.

The story of how Millie got that rubbing is rather typical of how Millie often got what she wanted. She said she knew where the monument was and wanted to prove to the missionaries and

Chinese that Christianity was an ancient Chinese belief, not primarily a Western one. She determined to get a rubbing of it as soon as she could get to Sian. (A rubbing is done by placing black chalk on the stone itself, being sure it is in the wording, then laying fine rice paper over it, gently rubbing until it brings out a print.)

Friends in Hong Kong warned her that it would be very expensive, if they did have one; and she probably could not afford it. She was not deterred. When she got to Sian, saw the stone, read the Chinese part, and ascertained that it was the Nestorian Monument, she asked the people if they had any rubbings because she said, "I would like to buy one."

"No, no, no," they exclaimed.

"Oh, come on now," she answered, "this is a very special stone. I would very much like to have a rubbing."

Again they repeated, "No, no."

"If you did have one, how much would it cost?" she asked.

"Oh, at least 50 Hong Kong dollars," they responded.

"Good," she said, "but I have to prepare because I don't have that much money with me." (50 Hong Kong dollars are worth 80 U.S. dollars.)

A man standing back behind the counter, watching Millie intently, came up to her with a smile.

"Now understand," he said, "we don't know if we have a rubbing or not, but just in case we do, I will go and look on the shelves for it. If we have it, I will bring it to your hotel rooms."

"Fine," she said, "I will change the money tomorrow, and have it ready for you."

Sure enough, he came the next night to her hotel with the rubbing. She laid it out on the floor to check it, and to be sure it was what she wanted. She only got one side, the Chinese writings,

not the names of the missionaries in Syriac. She was well pleased
to get any of it.

Millie and the rubbing of the Nestorian Monument

As she gave him the money, she told him she would like to
give him a book to express her thanks if he would like to receive it.
Then she laid a new Chinese script New Testament in his hand. He
turned in wonder and asked, "Is it a Bible?"

"Yes," she replied, "the part called the New Testament."

He broke into a wonderful smile and said, "I am delighted to
have it. Thank you so much."

Millie carried that long unwieldy thing all over America on her
next furlough. All of us had to hear about the Nestorian
monument. Later she had it mounted on a scroll and gave it to the
Hong Kong Baptist Seminary. They have it hanging under glass in

their main front hall. May Christianity never die out in China again!

Bringing Bibles Into China

When Millie felt it was safe for her Chinese friends to be visited by a foreigner and a missionary, she started looking for them, and she started bringing in some Bibles to them. The Chinese had started printing some Bibles from old plates that had been saved, but they could print relatively few to meet the great need. Folks had to sign up for some time before they were able to buy one. Very, very few Bibles had survived the Mao years.

Millie's method was to openly carry them unwrapped in a tote bag where they could easily be seen, or to place them at the very top of her clothes in the suitcase where they would be spotted the minute the luggage was opened. In America, I was hearing how hard it was to smuggle Bibles into China so I was amazed that Millie never seemed to have any trouble walking in with them in full view.

On my trip with Millie in 1982, I saw how it worked. Before our departure from Hong Kong into China, we went to the Bible Book Store where Millie bought several Chinese Bibles, a Bible Atlas, a concordance, two or three other Bible reference books, and paperback hymn books. She placed some of these in the top of her suitcase, until it would hardly close and was quite heavy. She asked me to take the others.

"I don't have any room in my suitcase." I exclaimed. I had just brought a small case and a flight bag along. Both were full!

"Well," she replied, "you can just carry the rest of the books in the heavy plastic bag that they are in now."

"Mildred," I was horrified, "This bag says Bible Book Store in both English and Chinese!"

"That's all right," she said. "Just bring it along."

Buying Bibles at the Hong Kong Bible Book Store

Well, Millie may have been used to carting Bibles openly around China, but I was not. It gave me an uneasy feeling. In fact, with the bag I carried, I seemed to be advertising!

We had no problems or even comments when our luggage was checked. They were more interested in our wristwatches and cameras. This made me feel a little easier. Just a little!

We first toured Beijing. Among our trips to the Great Wall, the Hidden City, and Mao's tomb, Millie had set it up with the guide to take us to one of the open churches (even though it wasn't Sunday) to meet her friend, the pastor. I think the guide was a little dubious, but she brought us to the church. The pastor greeted Millie warmly and invited all of us to have tea. While we were there, Millie presented the pastor with a Reference Bible as the cautious guide watched but said nothing. The pastor was very pleased and grateful. Later, I questioned Millie about giving the pastor the Bible so obviously in front of the Communist guide. She explained that this way there would never be any doubt or suspicion of either the pastor or herself, or of what she had given him since the government guide was a witness to it all.

This was Millie's pattern and soon our national guide was quite used to it. In Chengdu, we visited the open church and the newly begun seminary. Several young men and women were now able to study for the ministry in this far western city. Their meager "library" consisted of only twenty to twenty-five books! How happy the teaching pastors and students were to receive the Bible Atlas, the Concordance, and the other reference books. Now, I understood why Millie had bought them.

Three other tour members had been given plain, small, untitled Bibles to smuggle into China. They had been told to hide them in their clothing, which they had done. They were so impressed with the young people and the work at the seminary, that they brought out their Bibles to leave there in Chengdu. Reluctantly, the seminary dean explained that he could not accept them. They were only allowed to have Bibles and Christian books that were clearly titled on the outside cover. It didn't make any difference if they were the newly-printed Bibles from Nanking in China, or if they came from outside the country, but they had to say plainly "Holy Bible" or even "Good News For Modern Man." The guide agreed. We had to take the unmarked Bibles back with us.

In our old, West China home city that is now named Losan, we visited our old mission house beside the Min River, a tributary of the mighty Yangtze. We also visited the big Buddha built into a huge cliff. There was no open church, and Millie knew of no Christian group there, but she found out in Chengdu the name of the old pastor, who was still alive and lived near his old church. As we traveled in the city, the local West China guide and Millie got out of our bus and asked the old people if they remembered the old Baptist church and knew where it had been. Most of the folks on the street didn't know, but they were happy to report that the Canadian church would be opened that very year.

Finally someone was able to tell them the section of Losan where they thought the Baptist Church had been. When our bus got to that area, Millie and the guide again got off the bus and asked if anyone knew where the old church was. It was just a block away! Then they asked if anyone knew where the old pastor lived, and they named him.

"Yes," said one older man, "but why ask us? That's his son standing right over there!"

Isn't God's timing and placement sometimes amazing? Sure enough, the pastor's son was right there, and he took us to see his father. We went through a rather makeshift silk factory that was built right into the old church. The sanctuary was a place of storage for the bolts of silk. We went up some rickety stairs to a small two-room apartment where the pastor lived with his wife, his son, daughter-in-law, and their child. The pastor was confused by our visit. He had spent several years in prison, and he had had a stroke. It was a little while before he knew who we were. Then he got very excited and said, "Your father built our church. Your father built our church." He was right. Papa was an engineer as well as a missionary. He had, indeed, built this church.

The Church in Losan - second from left is the pastor

Before we left the old pastor, Millie wanted to give him the hymnbooks, but he was afraid to receive them. His son urged him to accept them, but still he was very reluctant. Then suddenly, and surprisingly, the guide declared,

"We have heard all over town that the Canadian church will open this year. When it opens you will need to have hymn books. Please take them."

The pastor took the books.

Two interesting things happened because of our visit that day. The immediate result was that the old, disgraced, jail-bird pastor was suddenly held in honor. Many people on the streets were watching. One has to respect a man who has foreign dignitaries (us), and a government representative (the guide) come all this way just to visit him!

The second result was that our father's old building was the church they opened that year by moving out part of the silk factory. Four years later when I returned, the whole silk factory was gone; the pastor, with his health miraculously restored was back preaching in his pulpit; and Losan again had a church in their city where people could find the Lord. They had even sent a young man to seminary in Chengdu, preparing to come back as a fellow pastor. Praise God!

Millie eventually got rid of the unmarked Bibles. I don't know where. I do know what happened on another trip when people brought in the unmarked Bibles. Millie talked to a Bible Woman who not only taught in the local open church, but also had Bible classes in the rural villages where there were no open churches. She said the village people would be glad to have any kind of Bible, and she took them.

I brought my empty Bible Book Store plastic bag home with me in my suitcase to show people in America how we openly "smuggled" Bibles into China.

The Man in the Picture

Missionary Eleanor Tate was amazed at how Millie could find people, even ones she did not know but had been writing to. In one case, Millie didn't even have a name, just a picture of a man and the city he lived in. This is how Eleanor explained the situation:

"I went with Millie on a tour in China that included Guilin. Before we left, one of the young men in Hong Kong gave Millie a Bible and a picture. The snapshot was of himself, a young man, and a tour guide. The young man in the center had asked for a Bible. Millie took the Bible and put the picture in her wallet. Our small tour group took the scenic raft trip along the Lejiang River past all the beautiful, unusual rock hills near and in Guilin. Along the way, we stopped to climb one of these hills. At the top, I wandered around looking for good photo spots. When I came back to a picnic type area, there was Millie sitting at a table with a Chinese guy, looking at the photograph together. He was the third person, the guide, in the picture *and she had recognized him!* Imagine running into him on that river peak and actually remembering him from the picture!

In Guilin, Millie actually found "the man in the picture"!

"He said she was right - he was that person! She asked if he remembered the other young chap in the center. He said he did. He was attending the university in Guilin. Then she asked if he would take the Bible to him. He declined, not wanting as a tour guide to get involved. However, he added, 'There is another fellow up here today from the university, maybe he will take the Bible to him.' The guide called the student over, and he said that he would be glad to deliver it to him!"

Talk about God's guidance!

Belinda

Like Millie, I also received a gift in China when I was very young and returning to America on furlough. Not a rabbit like Millie's Clarence, but a doll.

I was sad and a little frightened. Missionary children often don't know where "home" is. I was not happy to be leaving China to go to that foreign place that people were calling "home in America". A Chinese lady made me a beautiful rag doll I called Belinda, to comfort me on the long voyage home. It was a very nice gift for a little four-year-old who felt lost.

Some people have not agreed with me about Belinda being beautiful. She does have a rather flat body, and a flat hairless head. She came with an obviously patched right arm. When I was growing up she lost her original mammy outfit, her red cotton nose, and most of her mouth. A friend grabbed her one day and ripped her face so that she has a rather long sewed-up scar right up to her white, button eyes. I'm afraid she has now been sewed in many other places, too. In these later days, some rather cruel folk have even suggested that she looks like E.T. Well, maybe, a little bit, but she is beautiful to me.

I had other dolls, but Belinda is the one I kept. I don't know why. I took her with me to summer camps, to college, and even on my honeymoon. Poor Al!

Although usually Belinda is at home, she has enjoyed many a Baptist House Party and Women's Conference. As I have been a counselor at summer camps, I have always put Belinda on the pillow as soon as I made the bed. She is so unusual that people ask where I got her, and why she is with me. She breaks the ice very fast.

"Who brought that old doll?" is a comment I have heard several times. And the whispered answer, "She belongs to the *counselor!*"

When I was packing to go with Papa and my sister-in-law, Viola, to Hong Kong for Papa's 90th birthday, I wanted to travel light. I decided to only take a small suitcase and a flight bag. We were actually going not only to the birthday party that Millie was planning in Hong Kong, but all around the world. Millie was joining us for the rest of the trip on her way home for a furlough.

My daughters, Faith and Charity, were watching me pack. "Where is Belinda?" they asked. I explained that on this trip I didn't have room for her.

"Take out some of the clothes and put Belinda in," Faith insisted. "She needs to go 'home' to China, too!" The girls put her safely in my suitcase.

When we got to Millie in Hong Kong, she thoroughly agreed with Faith and Charity. She insisted that we take special pictures of Belinda so that the girls would know she didn't spend all her time in the suitcase. Millie snapped pictures of Belinda in a little moon festival cart in Macau, Belinda looking at Communist China from the New Territories in Hong Kong, Belinda visiting the Royal Palace in Bangkok, Belinda in a park in Singapore, Belinda meeting a sacred cow in India, Belinda on a fortress in Afghanistan, Belinda on a Crusader Castle in Jordan, and so forth. Sometimes Papa, Viola, or I would take the pictures and Millie would hold Belinda. Of course, the people who saw us taking pictures of an old doll, thought we were either strange or foolish.

Belinda in the Moon Festival Cart

We had a funny little incident happen when we were in Nelore, India. A nice Christian man drove us around to see the Lone Star Church, the hospital, and the schools. We continued to take pictures, often holding Belinda. At the Baptist Girls School, he introduced us to his wife who was a teacher there. Then he excused himself as he talked privately to his wife. She shook her head. He came back and apologized that his wife had none of her homemade dolls right now. He said she made beautiful ones. He wanted to send me a new doll in America as soon as his wife could make one. He had an awfully hard time believing that Belinda was precious to me, and that I didn't need a new doll.

Later (in 1982), Millie said it was now possible to travel all the way to Losan, China, the place where we had lived. She planned a tour for family and missionary friends. This time, my brother, Norman, as well as his wife, Viola, came on the tour. As soon as it seemed that I would be able to go, Faith and Charity were already insisting that Belinda go, too. After all, she only really got to see *China* on the last trip. This time, we would get all the way "home" where the Chinese lady lived who made her. Even my husband, Al, thought she ought to make this trip.

Millie and I again took Belinda out for pictures: Belinda at the Ming tombs, Belinda at the Temple of Heaven, Belinda in the rain on the Great Wall .... Our poor guides weren't so sure about us!

However, when we got to Western China, our local guide was fascinated. He wanted to know all about the doll, especially who made her. I had to tell him I didn't know; it was some friend of Mother's. He insisted that we must try to find her old friends. "We must find someone who knows who made the doll."

"I don't think that is possible," I explained. "She was made in 1932, fifty years ago." That did not deter him. Our guide took pleasure in finding many old Christian friends that had known our folks. He took us to homes, to churches and even to the newly-opened seminary in Chengtu. He was the guide who told the pastor in Losan to take the hymn books. (Normally a guide was considered to be a Communist, and they usually discouraged groups from going to a church or meeting Christians.)

When we only had a part of one day left, he was disappointed because he had found many people that knew our folks, but not one that knew about Belinda. However, he said he had found an old Bible Woman who would meet us at the Chengtu church in the morning before we had to leave.

Miss Hu Kai Hsiang did meet us in the morning. Millie was pleased that she remembered Mother so well. In due time, Millie told me to bring Belinda out of her little bag, and she showed the doll to Miss Hu. Miss Hu took Belinda in her hands and said, "My this is a very old doll; she was made in 1932 by Mrs. Wong."

I didn't understand what they were saying because they were speaking Chinese but the guide who was sitting next to me, got very excited. He turned to me, and said in English, "She knows who made the doll, she knows who made the doll!" And then, he started interpreting what Miss Hu was saying. Miss Hu, Mrs. Wong and Mother used to travel to villages outside of the city to tell people about Jesus. She talked about some of their experiences and how they always had to wait for Mrs. Wong because she had bound feet and could not walk well. She was a poor widow woman who wore only black clothes. I guess Belinda was made from one of her old dresses. I always wondered why a Chinese doll was black. It was probably all she had.

Edie and Belinda. We found Miss Hu Kai Hsiang who remembered Mother and knew Mrs. Wong who made Belinda

The guide was so pleased. He had accomplished his purpose. We were even more pleased because, not only had he found out about Belinda, but also he had introduced us to so many Christians in Chengtu and Losan. Besides being able to greet them and encourage them, Millie brought presents of Bibles, commentaries and hymnbooks for them which they were glad to receive.

I'm sure that when Mrs. Wong made a rag doll for a four-year-old child, she had no idea how long the "child" would keep her, or that the doll would open so many doors for us fifty years later.

You may have heard Millie tell this story when she came back to America. It was a favorite of hers and, of course, she kept up with Miss Hu and visited her every time she went to Chengtu.

Is Belinda still traveling? Of course! On one of our recent trips, our luggage was left in Australia after we had arrived in New Zealand. My husband asked, "Is there anything irreplaceable in our luggage?" I anxiously told him, "Belinda is still in Australia!" Luckily our luggage caught up with us the next evening. Belinda's latest trip was to see our granddaughter's wedding in southern Illinois.

What have I learned from Belinda? Never to think anything I do is unimportant to God. He can take the smallest things and use them not only for the moment, but for a lifetime, and longer.

"But God hath chosen the foolish things of the world to confound the wise, and God hath chosen the weak things of the world to confound the things which are mighty" (I Cor. 1:27).

A Catholic Church by the River

Traveling with Millie was always an adventure for me. Once on a three-day boat trip down the Yangtze River, our Christian tour group stopped at different river towns to do some shopping. On one occasion, we docked in the late afternoon and walked up to the main shopping area which was mostly just sidewalk shops and people with their wares going among us trying to get us to buy. Many of us had already bought more than we could easily carry. I was trying to manage both a flute and a Chinese violin.

A lady came up to one of our Taiwan missionaries and whispered in Chinese, "We have a home church here, and we would like you to come and visit."

The missionary told Millie about this request, but by that time the Chinese lady had disappeared into the crowd. Millie told the guide that our group would like to visit the house church, but that we would have to ask people in the crowd where it was. Our national guide by this time was used to such strange requests. She and Millie asked many people where the house church was. They either did not know, or did not tell. However, several mentioned that there was a newly-opened Catholic church farther up the hill. Since we couldn't find out anything more about the home church, Millie decided we should go to see the Catholic one.

The woman who answered the gate to the Catholic compound was very afraid. She ran quickly to get the priest. He was also afraid. Millie told him we were Christian friends, and the guide explained that this was not an official visit or any kind of censure, just American tourists who wanted to see his now-opened church.

The priest seemed a little less wary after this explanation, yet he was still very reluctant to show us the chapel. He said it was just a plain building. All of the beautiful statues and fancy gold leaf work were gone. In fact, there wasn't a picture of a saint or anything where we could even light a candle. When he remembered the beauty of the sanctuary before the church had been closed, and all of the things that had been taken away, he felt very sad and bereft. He felt God must be very sad, too!

Millie explained that we were Protestants. Most of our churches would seem very plain to him. We just wanted to rejoice with him that Christ could again be worshipped openly in this place. Hesitantly he took us into the chapel. It was newly-painted and nice. We liked it. One of our group started singing a hymn. We all joined in and sang several hymns. Surprisingly, the priest hummed and sang a little, too, in Chinese. I was amazed he knew any of the songs. Where had he learned them in the years of persecution? It was always better not to ask.

Several in our group joined in short prayers of thanksgiving to God (mainly in English, but some in Chinese), praising Him for this now-opened place, and asking for God's continued blessing on the work and on the priest. When we opened our eyes again, I was amazed at the way the priest looked. Radiant! What a change! Several of our group took pictures of the priest and Millie and others before we left. I'm sure his church would never seem so plain to him again. The priest begged us to stay longer, but it was time for us to get back to our boat.

When I look at the pictures of this priest, I am again reminded of his happy glowing face and the feeling of God's special Presence there.

The Presence of God is the best decoration a church can ever have.

A Sunday in Tibet

Millie had prayed diligently to get back into China for so long that when opportunities came, she always jumped at the chance. She had many very specific places she wanted to go to get in touch with Christians she knew, or knew about, but she was also fascinated by any place in China. By 1980, the travel bureau in Hong Kong knew they had a steady client. When China Travel was able to book a tour to Tibet and needed another tourist on the trip, they invited Millie to go along. She gladly agreed, though she had to really scrimp to get the money. Most of the travelers were tourists from America, England or France. Few people even in China had ever had the chance to go so far West in what was now a part of their own country, so a few privileged mainland Chinese were joining the tour in Beijing.

Before the 1950's, when the Communists took it, Tibet had been an independent country ruled by a Buddhist Lama. It had different customs and a different language. Southern Baptists had never served there; no Christian group had been welcome. Millie wondered if there were any Christian literature in the Tibetan language. The Bible Society directed Millie to the Overseas Missionary Fellowship (the former China Inland Mission). Their staff found three old Tibetan tracts and they Xeroxed four copies of each - twelve tracts in all. Way too few!

When Millie got there, she knew there were no churches in Tibet so she knew there would be no chance or place to worship on Sunday, but she decided to dress up anyway. She put on a long , quite fancy batik dress. When she got on the bus in the morning, the fellow travelers noticed. One man whistled. They asked "Oh, why are you so dressed up today?" She said, "This is Sunday, and this is the only way I could think to honor the day since we will have no chance to go to church here." One of her fellow tour members said, "Trust us who are heathen, to not even remember it is Sunday."

Since she had the long skirt on, she did not want to cross a little stream on stepping stones to get to a small Buddhist temple. She did not wish to get her dress wet. So instead, she just walked along, talking to various people who understood Chinese. A Tibetan priest in his saffron robes came toward her, and he asked her, "Will you open your umbrella?" Millie was rather amused and found this interesting. She had one of the fold-up umbrellas that you press a button and it opens itself. He thought it was quite magical. She showed him how she did it, and then she said to him, "Sir, I have a little gift that I would like to give to you, but I want you to understand that it is about faith, and maybe it isn't convenient for you to receive it. So I don't want you to think that just because a foreigner gives it to you, you have to receive it. It's up to you. Maybe you would rather not receive it." By this time he was getting very curious, and he wondered what this foreign lady wanted to give him. She pulled out a tract that had a picture of a man with a heavy load, and then it had a picture of the man going up a hill toward a cross, and then a picture of the man kneeling at the foot of the cross, and the heavy burden was falling off. The last picture showed the man leaving his burden at the cross and walking away very happily. The four pictures were on one side and Tibetan writing was on the other side.

She gave him the tract, and he looked at it with quite a lot of interest. She saw from his face that he was very puzzled; he didn't know what the cross meant. She thought, "He doesn't know anything about this." A little boy was standing beside her, and he held out his hand as if he wanted something, too.

The priest started to read the tract out loud. Immediately, as he read, there were about twelve people surrounding him. He would read about three sentences, and then he would turn the tract over and point to the picture of the man with the heavy burden. Everyone would nod in agreement. He read a little farther and turned it over again to the picture, and everyone would nod.

By this time, Millie was watching but sort of standing at the far edge of the crowd, listening to the priest read in Tibetan. The little boy continued to stay by her expectantly. While all this was going on, she heard a voice beside her asking in Chinese, "Is it a Protestant tract or a Catholic tract?"

Millie answered, "Well, I guess you could say it's a Protestant tract, but are you a Catholic?"

It was a young Chinese soldier standing there, and he smiled the most engaging smile at her and said, "Yes, I'm a Catholic."

She said, "Isn't it nice and special that you, a Catholic, and me a Protestant, can think about Jesus Christ in Llasa (Tibet) today, and we can praise Him?"

The soldier said, "Yes, that's wonderful. I'd like to tell you some good news."

"Oh, I'd love to hear some good news", she replied.

They were whispering while the Tibetan priest continued to read the tract, and point to things in the picture.

The young soldier said, "I am from Yunan Province, and in my hometown the church has been re-opened again, and they are having services in the building. The people can now worship God openly. Isn't that good news?"

"That's wonderful news," she said, "Great!"

Then suddenly her tour group returned. "Oh, oh, I'm going to have to fade out of this picture," she thought, so she whispered to the young soldier, "I'm going to have to go now, but may the joy of the Lord be in your heart always, and God's peace be with you!"

And he answered, "May His peace be with you, too!"

Then she quickly turned away. The small boy was still beside her with his hand held up toward her. She finally gave him one of her precious tracts. He was so happy; he took it and ran away.

When Millie was about thirty yards away, she turned back and looked at the people. The young soldier was waving his hand and smiling. The priest was still reading his tract, and the crowd standing around him were still nodding their heads as she got on the bus, and they drove away.

Millie said she gave another of her precious tracts to an insistent little boy later on in the week. She felt maybe they thought the words were from the Dali Lama, and she wondered if she had wasted those two precious Tibetan tracts.

But I felt differently. I told her that on that very special Sunday, the tract that she gave to the little boy might have been the most important thing she did. God often uses such small things to further His plans. I wondered if the tract was for the little boy, or if he was going to bring it to someone else who was seeking a message from God, someone like Cornelius or the Ethiopian treasurer that we learn about in the Bible book of Acts.

On the Silk Road

Millie first became interested in the Silk Road when some of her students were sent to far away North West China. The Silk trade route was over high mountains, the Gobi desert and large uninhabited areas. Chinese and even Japanese traveled these difficult trails to get to India and the Mideast. Nestorian Christians traveled this route to get to China. Amazing! One of her old Guilin students, Jimmy, that she knew well, was living by the Silk Road.

Millie was also writing to Margaret who taught English at the large university in Urumqi. Actually, Margaret was an Eurasian who had lived in Shanghai and was one of Elizabeth Ward's Sunday School children. After Elizabeth died, Millie started writing to her, and they became friends.

Millie took her first tour on the Silk Road in 1983. Even though Urumqi was so far inland, Millie thought it was now safe to write to both Margaret and to Jimmy telling them she was coming and hoped to meet them. Margaret was very enthusiastic; but she did not get a reply from Jimmy. Missionary teacher and friend, Eleanor Tate, went along with Millie on this Silk Road journey.

As the tour headed west, they went by overnight train to Lanzhou and then to Dunhuang on an old, Russian propeller plane with bald tires. In this part of China, there are vast deserts with small cultivated spots. They took a camel ride out to huge sand dunes, but they walked back and found it was hard going in the loose, dry sand. Two Chinese visitors, members of a sports group, came to help Millie. The girl said to her in Mandarin, "Can you understand my words?"

Millie answered, "I think so."

The girl then surprisingly shared, "Would you believe that my mother and sister are Christians?"

"What about you?" Millie asked.

She said, "I'm not a believer yet."

The young man stated, "Oh, there aren't many Christians left in China now."

But the girl answered, "There certainly are - millions of them!"

Millie was able to give the girl a Gospel.

Xinjiang Territory actually comprises one-sixth of China, but there are very few Chinese there. Most of the people in this sparsely-settled area are Uighurs, a Turkish ancestral group who speak a Turkish sounding language. Urumqi is the only city and the main place where Chinese live with the Uighur population.

When the tour arrived in Urumqi, the local guide had his tour planned for the city, and he did not consider it good for foreign visitors to get too close to the Chinese or the Uighur people. Millie was more careful around him, and did not at first even let him know she spoke Chinese. On travel forms, when it says to name your friends in China, Millie always left it blank; she never filled it in. She insisted that the guide include the Xinjiang University in his city tour. After all, they had brought two cartons of books from Hong Kong Baptist College for the University. Included in these cartons were some Good News Bibles. Millie did not try to hide them, but as usual, carried them openly. The government officials never seemed to worry about them, in fact sometimes, they seemed pleased.

The guide was puzzled and reluctant; he had not had this problem before (people suddenly donating books to his university). Millie told him about Professor Margaret who taught English and was expecting to receive the books. He told her, "She has left; she is not here. She has gone to Peking."

Millie insisted, "I've written to her, and she knows we are coming."

The guide replied, "No, no, no, no, she is not here."

Millie pressured him, "But we *are* going to the University. We *are* going to deliver the books." Because she was so persistent, he finally agreed to take them in the afternoon.

When they got to the University, Millie spoke to the public relations officer in Chinese. He made the comment that he had sent for Margaret, and she would be coming soon. She had been waiting for word from Millie all morning. The disconcerted guide said he'd thought she had gone to Shanghai (before he had said Peking). In just fifteen minutes, Margaret was there, greeting Millie as a very special friend. She was so pleased with the books in English that she could use in her classes, including the Good News Testaments.

Margaret arranged for Eleanor Tate to give a lecture to her English majors. She talked to them about Shakespeare's *King Lear*. Eleanor was surprised at how few books and teaching materials were available. She was glad Millie brought the books. When Eleanor returned to Hong Kong, she sent over twenty packages of books to Margaret to help in teaching her classes.

Later that week, Margaret invited the tour group to her home for a meal. It was there that her other special friend, Jimmy, found Millie. He did not live in Urumqi and had traveled 300 miles (16 hours by train) to come and see her! How wonderful it was for Millie to see him again! She had prayed for him for thirty-four years.

With another guide, the group traveled way out in the minority country near Dunwan to see a pagoda in the middle of a rice field. Tour members from Alabama were interested in the cotton fields that reminded them of home. As they walked along, Millie heard music and saw decorations on a farmhouse and saw people milling about. She could tell it was a wedding. She crossed the street where she could see a man inside making noodles, a traditional food of good fortune and long life for weddings. Millie asked if she could bring her friends to watch him. He said, "Oh yes, welcome to our wedding." The guide was very pleased that his foreign tour could see the wedding celebration, and the lovely bride in her traditional *red* gown - red for happiness.

The groom came out and welcomed them and invited them into the house where people were sitting on stools before square tables and eating noodles. Millie asked if they could take pictures and when they agreed, she took several. Later, Millie sent pictures of the wedding back to the couple. They were so very pleased. Because these foreigners had "crashed" the wedding, the bride and groom had wedding pictures they otherwise would not have had.

Millie returned to the area in 1993. She hoped to stop at the farmhouse and greet the couple, but they had no time. They briefly stopped in Dunwan where the groom just happened to be in town and recognized her. He invited the whole tour group to his home. He proudly said he now had two sons (minority people are allowed three children instead of only the one allowed Han Chinese.) They were unable to accept his invitation, but Millie was glad for even this brief encounter with someone else who had become her friend.

A Letter From an Old Friend

As Millie found her Guilin friends, they in turn told others where she was. In this case, one of Millie's Guilin students found her. Someone must have given him her address. He wrote her this letter in English on August 19, 1982:

Dear Miss Millie Lovegren:

I was a student of the English Holy Bible class of the Baptist church in Guilin in 1948-1949. My name is Jia-hua Chen.

Up to now we have long separated for over thirty years. How long to see you again I am! as well as Mr. Loden and Mrs. Loden.

In 1952, I was admitted to civil department of Qinghua University of Peking after an examination. After graduated, I left Northeastward and reached Guilin after passing through many different places.

Now I, as an engineer, go in for architectural design in Guilin Garden Bureau. Several plans which were designed by me, have been adopted at "Seven Stars Cave", "Reed Flute Cave", "Elephant Hill Park" and so on.

Yesterday, Mr. Pao Tsun-chuan at his home baptized my two brothers, Chen Jia-ji, and Chen Jia-qi. The former, who graduated from Qinghua University in 1961, and the latter, who graduated from Qinghua University in 1964, work at Peking.

For ten years period of "the Great Proletarian Cultural Revolution" - on those days I was thrown in to prison.

I miss God all the time! I miss you and Mr. Lodens very much! Day and night I look forward to your coming.

Now I send an invitation that you visit Guilin when you are at the right moment. I will keep you company to go sightseeing scenic spot.

Because I miss Mr. Lodens very much. Please tell me Mr. Loden's address, if you know.

I wish to meet you very much. Please write return to me.

Sincerely yours,

Engineer Jia-Hua Chen

Guilinshi Garden landscape

Bureau, Guilin, Guangxi,

People's Republic of China

A Day Trip into China

By 1984, Millie had been going into China regularly, sometimes on long tours, but usually just a quick trip to churches in Canton or a visit to a friend near the border. She did not fear being in China, and she wanted to see the Chinese Christians on both sides of the border cooperating with each other.

When cousins, Dick and Pauline Chauran, visited Millie in Macau for three weeks, they looked at a picture of the gate that separated Portuguese Macau from Communist China and thought of all the years that the gate was closed for most people. Now Millie wanted to take them through that gate into China to look at some property that she wanted to rent. She thought it would be interesting for the Baptist ladies of Macau to have a retreat inside China! This is the way our cousins described their day trip into China:

> Several of Millie's friends joined us on this quick, one-day tour. It was spooky for us going through the guarded gate. We knew that the people of China had more freedom now, and yet there was a feeling of repression and extreme carefulness, so as not to offend anyone. Later that evening when we came back through the gate into Macau, we had a feeling of great relief and relaxed freedom. We didn't know if anyone there was going to stop us, and they didn't, but we knew they could have if they wanted to. Many of the returning Chinese were thoroughly interviewed making sure, I guess, that they were really from Macau.
>
> We found the town of Shikay very interesting. There were open one-man shops right on the sidewalks. A man was fixing a bicycle tire, next to him a man was picking chicken feathers, and right next to him a man was cutting hair. When the barber was through he picked up his stool and walked off. No clean up. I guess the hair just stayed there until it blew away.

We stopped at the church in Shikay on our way to see the retreat property. Millie knew the four pastors of this church - three men and a Bible woman. This combination of pastors was much more unusual than most - a Baptist, a Methodist, a Catholic, and a Mormon! People who are starved for anything Christian learn to bend a long ways. The Bible was their only teaching book allowed.

Millie asked two of the pastors to order some dinner for our group (18 or 20 of us) so that we could eat there when we returned. They agreed. We were gone for a few hours up to the place where the campground was located. There was an old church that had kind of been made into a seminary with only one student so far. They were willing to rent the area for a retreat.

When we got back to Shikay we found our dinner had been prepared for us - on a brand new, six level, all restaurant boat on the Pearl River! It was obviously a place for tourists from outside of China. It was very fancy! Millie invited the two pastors to eat with us and they accepted and brought their families. Now we were thirty people. We were there eating for about three hours. We never got through all thirty courses of the meal. We certainly had never expected to eat so royally.

When we were done I asked the girl that served all this meal if I could give her a tip. She answered, "No." In China, tips are considered bad. Everyone should be thankful for what they make and not be greedy! I then asked her if she could take an American dollar bill as a souvenir. She again said, "No, but I would like to see one."

When it came time to pay, Millie didn't have enough money. I had just cashed two one-hundred dollar travelers checks the day before in Macau. It took all of that, and I don't know how much more - at least the money that I had and all that she had, and I don't know if others also helped pay the bill.

There was a pilot on the boat who could speak a little English. I talked to him for awhile and then reached in my pocket, where I had a Gideon New Testament. I asked him if he would like an American New Testament. He just grabbed it out of my hand. He probably wouldn't be able to read much of it at first, but hopefully he used it to learn more English. Can you think of a better text book in the world than the Bible?

Meeting Dr. Yang

While they were in Macau, Dick and Pauline took another trip into China with Millie because, they said,

She wanted us to go with her into China to visit Dr. Yang. Who was Dr. Yang? She didn't know! He had written a letter to the Southern Baptists in Hong Kong requesting a King James version of the Bible in large print. Somehow the letter's message was not clear, so they were not sure who he was, or what he wanted. They turned the letter over to Millie in Macau to see if she wanted to do anything about it. She did.

Dr. Yang lived at Tai Shan inside China, south of Macau and off the tourist routes. People didn't think Millie would be able to get a visa to go there, but she wanted to meet him and find out exactly what he wanted. Knowing that visas were not available for a certain area didn't stop Millie, it just slowed her down some. In this case, it only took a week and a little extra money. As soon as she found out she could take a little group of us to Tai Shan, she wrote Dr. Yang a letter and crossed the border into China to mail it to let him know we were coming.

Millie had us carry Bibles, song books, and Christian literature in our suitcases. They never checked. I asked the girl when we went through the customs house area, if she wanted me to open my suitcase because I had Bibles and things in there. She wasn't worried about it but she was concerned about our watches, cameras and electronic things. We had to register them and be checked to see that we still had them when we returned.

We were surprised to find a brand new hotel in Tai Shan built for businessmen. It was beautiful. Pauline decided to take a shower but found there was no water. In a little while, the water returned but she decided not to risk being in the middle of a shower and, again, having the water disappear. We asked for keys to our room and discovered that they had no idea where they might be. No one locked their doors.

The next morning the Chinese were having rice gruel for breakfast. Millie tried to get a more American breakfast for us. She asked for scrambled eggs. They only had three in the entire hotel kitchen. They fixed the three they had, and found some honey rolls for us. We also had tea and coffee. The first batch of coffee we had to send back because the waitress had written Irish coffee. We were surprised to be served coffee with whiskey in it.

Dr. Yang was afraid that it might not be safe for us to go to him, so he came to us. He was about sixty years old, an apparently well-educated man and a *bitter* one. I guess that wasn't surprising since he had been put in prison during the cultural revolution, and later he was sent to a forced labor commune where he was taught to think correctly (brainwashed). Even though he was now free, he couldn't practice "Western Medicine". He could prescribe Chinese herbal medicines that he had an expert knowledge of, but no operations for anything.

Dr. Yang's wife was a nurse. She could only find very lowly jobs because she also was branded as a traitor, a person with loyalties to foreigners (Southern Baptists). Before all this trouble, Dr. Yang and his wife had worked with a leper colony on an island off the China coast. He had saved his money and bought a junk (a small sailboat) so that he could sail up the coast to get medicines. The Southern Baptists had supported some of his work and encouraged him.

The Communists didn't really need an excuse for beating or jailing anyone, but they used his connections with Southern Baptists and his wealth (not only being a doctor, but owning a junk) as charges against him. They called him a "Capitalist Pig" and "a traitor".

Of course, after suffering as he had, it would be natural to be bitter at the Communist government, only that wasn't who Dr. Yang was angry at! He was bitter toward God! He felt he had been faithful and had tried to serve God well working among the lepers, but God had failed him. When he got out of prison, and finally back home from the forced labor of the commune, he wanted nothing to do with Christianity.

This very bitter man came home to a wife who felt the opposite. She had clung to her faith, prayed diligently for her husband, and tried to encourage others in their belief in Jesus. She even had little Bible meetings in their home. On certain nights when the people would come to worship, Dr. Yang would leave the house and walk around downtown.

He said three times he had walked to the police station to turn his wife in because of the Bible studies. Once he walked up to the officer at the desk, but he never actually reported her.

He was still bitter when we met him. He talked to us for three or four hours. Millie was certainly the right person to talk to him - so many of her Chinese friends had also been in prison. Millie's own missionary father spent almost five years in prison mainly in Chungking. Chinese Christians were sometimes very surprised to learn that Americans had also been taken captive and had suffered in prisons, just like themselves.

Before Dr. Yang left, we gave him the Bibles and the Christian literature that we had brought into China. Charles Mullins promised to send him the large print King James Bible that had been his original request.

His attitude had changed. He said at the door as he shook hands and walked out, "I'm the richest man in the world."

Dr. Joshua Yang

Later, Dr. Yang wrote several letters to Millie in English, which he knew and was no longer afraid to use. He explained he was not only reading the Bible carefully, but also listening to Bible classes in both Chinese and English on the radio. Millie encouraged missionary James Hollis to become Dr. Yang's friend. He brought the doctor Christian materials and other things he wanted. He was hungry to read anything about Christ in either Chinese or English. He even hoped to learn Greek so that he could study the Bible in its original language.

Dr. Yang was still not permitted to go to Tai Kim, the island leper colony, but he did get in touch with the present people who were in charge. He was happy to learn that after all this time there were twenty Christian lepers who had regular meetings. He sent them some of the Bibles, hymn books, and pamphlets that he had received. Some of the lepers started writing him and thanking him for the Bibles. They told him they were now singing hymns together and trying to witness to the other lepers.

Dr. Yang had a hard time trusting the open churches or their pastors. He felt the people in the village house churches were more zealous and spiritual. He asked for more Bibles and hymnbooks from the missionaries to give to the village people. He did not only want to be known as a Christian, but also as a Baptist, as he had been raised. He was happy now to remember the old, beautiful times of working together with Dr. N.A. Bryan, Miss Thelma Williams, and Miss Ruby Wheat in Yangchow.

He wanted his son to be a Baptist and hopefully study in America. He was in contact with the mission board and with William Carey College.

Dr. Yang wrote, "I am always joy, for I see the leading and mercy of my gracious Saviour. I read the Bible in my family to my wife. We are really grateful for God's lead through long, long tribulations from place to place, compelled to labor from field to coal mines, but now I taste the sweetness of Christ, as Jacob spoke in Genesis 28:16,17: *'Surely the Lord is in this place, and I did not know it. How awesome is this place! This is none other than the house of God, and this is the gate of heaven.'* I am not worthy to receive the blessing."

Millie and the Dedushka

At home in America on furloughs, Millie not only got acquainted with new family members through marriage, but also their families. Alan Bear, the brother of Evelyn Lambert, and brother-in-law of our son, Mark Lambert, was no exception. Millie visited Alan and his wife, Jan, in Oregon. Later something Millie did for a Russian man in Harbin, China, helped Alan and Jan in their marriage. This is the way they tell their story about "Millie and the Dedushka" (Russian for Grandpa):

The first time Jan Bear went to Liturgy in an Orthodox Church in Oregon, Alexei Shandar was there. Already 95, Alexei had been in America less than a year.

White-haired, white-bearded, slightly built, and despite his age standing as upright as the officer in the Tsar's army he once was, he chanted the Lord's Prayer in Church Slavonic and ended the prayer with a deep bow.

It was a step on a journey for both Alan and Jan. For Jan, that day was the discovery of something she'd hoped for, but had almost despaired of finding. For Alan, it was the beginning of a challenge to some of his most deeply-held, unexamined expectations.

Alexei's life had been long and eventful, as Jan learned later when she interviewed him to write an article for *The Orthodox Church* newspaper. Born in a small village in the Russian Far East, he had joined the Russian Army and served in World War I. He had continued fighting against the Bolsheviks in the Russian Revolution and had found himself in Kolchak's Ice March across Siberia, back into the Russian Far East.

He came to live in Harbin, a Russian city in China that had received the nickname "Moscow of the East". Before the Revolution, Russia had leased Harbin from China, an arrangement much like the lease on Hong Kong. Harbin was a city on the trans-Siberian railroad which provided a direct route from the main portion of Russia to Vladivostok on the Pacific Ocean. After the Revolution, many White Russians went to live in Harbin, and it continued to be a Russian city with a Russian mayor until the late 1920's.

But the Soviets had other matters to attend to, and they didn't spend much energy on Harbin, so the city reverted to Chinese control. But still the Russians and Chinese lived in harmony, if not unity, through World War II, when the Japanese held the area, until the Chinese Revolution. Then Alexei watched in dismay as the Maoists destroyed the city's old-style Orthodox cathedral, then saw Christian life more and more constricted under the Chinese. He bought an office building in 1960, too late to "own" it under the Communist government, and the Chinese took it "under management" which means that they functionally owned the building and gave Alexei a small salary to manage it.

In 1988, Alexei's last year in Harbin, the authorities decided to raze the building, claiming building code violations, even though it was in better shape than most of the structures people lived in.

Alla Matveenko, his step-daughter who lived in Forest Grove, Oregon, heard from a mutual friend that Shandar's health was failing. Through the help of some Americans, Alla made arrangements for Alexei to come to America. When it was nearly time for him to leave, the Chinese took away his Soviet passport. Although the Soviets had no great sympathy for the White Russians living in China, the people in the Soviet embassy were angry that the Chinese would take one of *their* passports, so they issued him a new one immediately. And he came to the United States.

He would die at the age of 100, well-loved, honored, and grateful to America and the people who helped him.

As Jan collected materials for the article that appeared in *The Orthodox Church* newspaper, she asked Alexei for photos. He brought one of himself as a dashing young man in 1928, another standing proudly in front of his office building in 1960, a few others - and one as an older man standing at a boat landing with a woman who looked familiar.

Jan looked at the picture and thought, "Who *is* that?" It must be someone famous, how else would she be recognizable? Corrie Ten Boom? No. Wait! It's Aunt Millie!

Millie Lovegren was one of the Americans who'd sponsored Alexei, making it possible for him to leave China.

Jan took the photo home and showed it to Alan. "Look at this photo," she said.

Alan studied the photo. He recognized Aunt Millie.

Jan's decision to embrace Orthodoxy had been a surprise even to herself. She was someone who'd not had much patience for church or ceremony most of her life, then she found in the Orthodox Church the structure and meaning she'd been looking for (with vestments and incense and a Liturgy that changes with the serene dignity of a prairie through the seasons).

As a lifelong Baptist, Alan was having trouble understanding his role as a husband and friend to his Orthodox wife. "We worship differently," he said, "sing differently and even seem to pray differently." Differences in church cultures and traditions - icons, the sign of the cross, formalities, incense, Communion practices, the length of the service, even terminology such as "liturgy" instead of "worship service," "homily" instead of "sermon," "Eucharist" instead of "Lord's Supper" - seemed incompatible.

But seeing Millie and Alexei together helped Alan realize that both he and Jan labor in love for the same God in Christ. "Millie's example has been very enabling, as I realized that we have, first, a Christian marriage and, second, an ecumenical one."

Jan remembers very clearly the moment Alan saw the photo. It was a turning point, from conflict to dialogue, from distrust to honest exploration of different points of view.

Alan and Jan have now adopted two Russian girls, and have provided them with a loving, Christian, though still ecumenical, home.

A Bell For Yibin

Once China started to reopen for foreigners to travel, Millie felt that encouraging the Christians in China was one of her most important jobs. So it was with a great deal of pleasure that she was not only able to go into China herself, but also was able to bring several former China missionaries back with her to the churches and the people where they had served. Thirty-five to fifty plus years had passed, yet many Chinese remembered their former young missionaries with fondness and welcomed them back gladly.

American Baptist Missionary, Astrid Peterson was 91 years old when she returned with Millie and their tour group to her Chinese field of service - the city of Yibin. Not only were the Chinese very happy to see her, but they thought her timing was wonderful. The church was open, and *their bell was back.* There was an article that went throughout China in the *Three Self Church Magazine* that told about the church and their bell. Astrid had a friend, Mrs. Daisy Tung, translate the article into English, as follows:

> In Yibin, Sichuan, there was a big, copper bell in the Yibin Christian Church. It was made in 1860 in Cincinnati, Ohio. The workmanship was very fine. It weighed 551 pounds. The inscription on the bell explains that it was given by the Baptist Church in Coffeyville, Kansas, and presented by their pastor, Rev. W. S. Upham, in 1886.

> When the bell was rung, the sound was clear and strong, so the whole city was able to hear it. Unfortunately, during the Communist revolution the bell was taken down and moved to a machine factory in the southern part of Yibin. (The church had been closed.)

> When the church was reopened, they started long negotiations about their bell. With the help of the Yibin Religion Department, the church got the bell back on August 19, 1993. The church and the Religion Department held a formal celebration on that occasion. The broadcast station of Yibin announced the news to the whole city. Thanks was given to the government, particularly to the Religion Department that assisted in the return of the bell.

> On August 25, 1993, Miss Astrid Peterson, an American missionary came back to visit the church in Yibin. When

she saw the bell she was exceedingly happy and pictures were taken of her and the bell.

Actually, I think Astrid was most pleased just to see her Chinese friends and the open church, but it was fun for her to be there just the week after they got their bell and join in their joy.

I'm sure that the pastor and all the people from Coffeyville, Kansas, who gave the bell in 1886 have gone on to be with Jesus in Glory, but it is nice to think that their gift, given so long ago to people so far away, continues to bring gladness to the Christians in Yibin, Sichuan, China.

Betty Brinerstall, like Astrid Peterson, returned to meet some of her old friends in China

Chapter Seven

RETIREMENT?

Millie had barely gotten home to America for retirement when she was asked to be the Interim Director of Student Ministries at the University of Idaho in Moscow. She accepted. She soon learned a lot about the challenges and difficulties which American students face. She also had a chance to bring foreign students into the group.

As soon as she was done there, she settled in our family home in Cherry Grove, Oregon, where she started a Women's Bible study and a Children's Bible club. She tried to get acquainted with her neighbors and succeeded well enough that official documents for the town came to her - some even said, "Miss Mildred Lovegren, Mayor of Cherry Grove". This is even more amazing since half of the time she was gone.

She also became interested in a Chinese group in Portland but it wasn't easy to work with them. They spoke Swatow - another Chinese language. She helped find them a Swatow-speaking minister.

Millie took college courses in Portland, McMinnville and in Australia. Yes, Australia! Rice University in Texas had a continuing studies program and tour, mostly in the Outback, to study and view Haley's Comet! At Lindfield College in Oregon she worked for a year and a half helping to prepare a Symposium on "American Missionary Movements' Impact on Chinese Society."

Millie spoke at House Parties from Virginia to Texas to Alaska. In Anchorage, she went to an Eskimo service where the folk looked so much like Koreans that she felt she was back home in Asia. She also spoke at conventions and summer camps. She even attended the Baptist World Alliance meetings in Argentina in 1995.

Of course, she took trips back to China. She was there leading a tour when the Tianamen Square riot erupted in Beijing. Suddenly all foreigners in the area were hurried away. Millie's tour was unable to complete their planned agenda and was sent on an alternate route. People at home in the United States lost track of her.

The Southern Baptist Convention was meeting in Las Vegas and a message was sent to the convention floor, "Stop and pray for Miss Mildred Lovegren who is lost in China!" The convention immediately did this, and many people were upset to know that their dear Millie was in trouble. Well, it's always very nice to be prayed for, but Millie's close friends found this message almost silly. Brother Parks, who had been Foreign Mission Board director for several years, commented, "Mildred Lovegren being lost in China, is as likely as B'rer Rabbit being lost in the Briar Patch!" Such was Millie's reputation for loving and wandering about China. She was simply at home again.

A New Generation

By the time Millie retired, China not only was allowing foreign tourists, but there were exchange programs that allowed missionaries to teach in a Chinese University for one or two years. Some Chinese professors were allowed to teach in Hong Kong or even Great Britain, Canada, or the United States. Chinese young people in increasing numbers were allowed to leave China for foreign universities.

Most of the missionaries that had come out with her on the S.S.Marine Lynx after World War II were now retired or had already gone on to Glory, including our parents. As she toured China in 1993, there was a measure of sadness as she heard reports of recent deaths in many cities of the old, old church leaders. Yet among the believers there was no panic. In each church there was already in place a young man, or woman, or both, newly seminary-trained and challenged to give a good witness for Christ.

She was seeing the "passing of an era", the "changing of the guard". Mr. Bill Hao, an old friend and leader of the Sichuan Christian Provincial Council, told Millie, "There are now sufficient seminary graduates to staff strong sponsoring churches and also to pay attention to the needs of weak churches, like Yaan." That was the new name of the city where we were born. The church was open, and had a small congregation, but as yet no pastor. On Sunday, they listened to taped sermons.

In Losan, where the church that papa built was located, the old pastor had died in the spring after God had given him ten good years back in his church. A fine young man that Millie had met several times in seminary in Chengtu, was now their pastor. He said to niece, Miriam Lanier, "Your father was a missionary, and your grandfather was a missionary. My father was a pastor, and my grandfather was a pastor. We need to be very faithful in serving our Lord too!" Miriam and her husband, Homer Lanier, are missionaries to the Arabs in Jerusalem. Miriam's father, our brother August, was a missionary to Jordan.

In this new generation, Millie felt she had two sons who were taking her place. Both were missionary kids who had come to Macau to work with youth in the two-year journeyman program. Both had returned to America to finish their seminary training. Both had married dedicated Christian wives and brought them back to the mission field with them.

The first special "son" was Tome Halsell, raised in Brazil so his natural language was Portuguese. How thankful Millie was to have him working with her from 1972 to 1974. Besides teaching in Pui Ching Middle School and helping her with the youth, he could also translate the Portuguese government documents and reach the young Portuguese soldiers.

Millie with Frances and Michael Halsell

When he and his wife, Frances, were first commissioned as missionaries, they were sent to Senegal, Africa. Then in 1981, they were sent to Hong Kong and Macau. Millie was so pleased to have Tome back and to get acquainted with Frances and their daughter.

Long after Millie retired, Tome and Frances were sent to Paris, France, to work with the overseas Chinese there. In 1993, Millie's Oregon friend, Sara Wisdom who had already taken several trips with Millie, said she had enough frequent flyer miles to get to Europe, and she hoped Millie did, too. She did! They headed for England, and then France. How wonderful to be with Tome and Frances again and with their two children, Christine and Michael. They now work with Chinese in Australia.

Her other special "son" was Steve Baker, who was born in Nazareth, Israel. He served as a journeyman from 1975 to 1977, teaching in Pui Ching Middle School and at the Macau Youth Center. She enjoyed working with him and said about him, "Steve is gifted in languages and music. He loves the Lord, and is at home with any people." He and his wife, Miranda, returned to Macau after Millie retired. They were so faithful in writing to Millie about all the events going on in Macau, and all the people she knew, that she still felt a part of the mission. Thank you, Steve and Miranda. Millie loved you guys, and was very proud of you. Keep up the good work for the Lord!

By Way of Calcutta

In 1990, Millie came down to San Bernardino, California for our Christmas Choir Cantata and then said she wanted to ride with us to spend Christmas week with our son, Jonathan, and his wife, Rhonda, and their family in Arizona.

"Of course," I said, "But you mean you want to ride both ways with us, don't you?"

"No," she replied, "I'm going back to Oregon by way of Calcutta."

Only Millie could say crazy things like that and be believed. Sure enough, she left Phoenix, Arizona for Calcutta, India to attend the Asia Baptist Youth Fellowship 8th Congress held January 7-14, 1991. A youth meeting at 71 years of age! Actually Millie and John Peacock were being honored as two of the folks who had worked for the birth of this fellowship in 1956. The first meeting was in Hong Kong. I guess Millie had been very instrumental in getting the groups together because she already had contact with several missionaries in several countries - not only Southern Baptist, but American Baptist, Conservative Baptist, Swedish Baptist (Baptist General Conference) and also some Canadian Baptists. Our own family was serving in three of these groups, and had grown up in the fourth.

Millie was asked to speak at an evening session on "The Joys and Difficulties of Being an Asian Christian." Millie's friend, Laura from Manilla, said she reminded the program planners that Millie was an American, but they had replied, "Only on the outside."

A special bonus for Millie was one day when many of the 400 youth delegates made a pilgrimage to nearby Serampore College established by William Carey, William Ward and Joshua Marshman in 1818. This is the school in India for which Millie had prayed for years, had given scholarships to students, and had asked professor friends to teach there for at least one semester. It is still training young people for the ministry today, as well as secular Christian pursuits. What a wonderful legacy from these early modern missionaries. May it continue to train future generations in India to serve Christ!

Sharing the Bible With Friends

When Millie wrote and told Hu Kia Shung, the Bible woman in Chengtu who knew our folks, that she was retiring, Miss Hu wrote back, "Your family does not retire from the service of the Lord. I am praying for the Lord to show you how to serve Him in America."

Millie later said, "I'm afraid she prayed me into a more difficult place than I'd experienced overseas."

Millie returned to the old family homestead in remote Cherry Grove, Oregon, in the hills between Portland and the coast. On furloughs, she had become aware of the uphill struggle most churches were having in the Northwest. It was reported that 70% of the people living in Oregon and Washington profess no religion at all! How very strange when they live in such a beautiful part of the country.

Millie at Cherry Grove

The Cherry Grove Baptist Church, the only church in town, had been invaded by a strange group who took over and pushed the local members out. Millie felt badly that a strange exclusive group had taken over the Baptist church building. After all, our grandparents had given the land and provided for the building. They had planned that the church would be the center of life and worship in Cherry Grove. For many, many years it was. But not now!

Millie looked around for ways she might witness in this spiritually bereft community. Doris Tornblade, a long-time Cherry Grove resident, wrote about a Bible study that Millie started with the women:

> We met at her house for a Bible study every week that she was in town. It was amazing that she would be gone so much of the time and then suddenly she would be back in Cherry Grove. She would call each one, and tell us she was home, and what day we could meet for Bible study. She didn't let us get away with staying home, even when we weren't feeling very well, because she would be disappointed if we weren't there. She was very encouraging.
>
> When we came traipsing up to her house at 10:00 a.m., she would have the coffee ready and something to eat. We visited for the first 15 or 20 minutes, and then we started our Bible study and prayer time. She liked to have us sing but it was hard because most of us had voices that were past singing - just gravel. Years ago, although I couldn't sing a tune by myself, I could follow, and my voice wasn't scratchy then.
>
> Millie studied so much just for us. She had lesson books for each one about Bible people or Bible books. One period of time we studied about the fruits of the Spirit. She talked slowly and distinctly, and explained the verses in our Bible Study clearly, so we could get the full benefit of it in terms we could understand. She had a fantastic memory.
>
> I will never forget her, and someday I will see her again!

The Children of Cherry Grove

Jane Person, another lady who had lived in Cherry Grove for many years, worked with Millie as they tried to tell the children of Cherry Grove about Jesus. She said,

I don't know how Millie met the local children. I guess she just talked to the ones she saw near her house, and they introduced her to others. Somehow she started a Bible Club for the children she knew after school once a week at her house. They would get off the bus at about 3:30, and we kept them until about 5:00.

"For over 5 years I played the piano, and assisted wherever I could, especially trying to keep the wiggly kids quiet while Millie was talking. She didn't know the newer choruses, so she taught them the ones she had learned as a child: "Jesus Loves Me," "Wide, Wide, as the Ocean," etc. Mainly we sang her favorite hymns. When she taught them "Holy, Holy, Holy," they liked it very much, but sang it rather irreverently. So then we had to teach them what the words meant. Another favorite of hers was "What a Friend We Have in Jesus.' The children enjoyed using her hymn books because each hymn was in Chinese as well as English. She read out of the King James Bible and then told a Bible story and had a prayer time. It was interesting to hear the prayer requests of the children.

Millie had lots of Kool-Aid for the children, and every week I brought big chocolate chip cookies. They always had to stay for the whole Bible study if they wanted a cookie.

Millie traveled so much that sometimes when she wasn't here, she would have someone else, like a pastor, come. Not everyone did well with the children, but we did like a lady from the Brookwood Baptist Church in Hillsboro. More often, we just waited until Millie got home and started the Bible Club again when she called.

It always amazed me that Millie who had never had
children of her own, wasn't upset if anything got moved
around or broken in her old house with so many
interesting things. She felt people were more important
than things. She made every effort to make the children
feel comfortable.

Millie, my husband Jim, and I took some of the children
to summer camp. At one camp they asked the young
people for their favorite song. A boy from Cherry Grove
said "Holy, Holy, Holy." The leaders tried to figure out
what chorus that was. They couldn't believe that these
youths knew and preferred hymns. After being taught by
Millie, they were sometimes on a different wave length
than most of the other young people.

The ones we took to camp were often the most troubled
kids. When we asked the leaders at one camp how they
did, they replied. "We couldn't say that they were no
trouble. Actually they required a little more work. But
we enjoyed them, and we think your kids really enjoyed
the camp."

Millie spent every Christmas with her family in
California, Georgia, or Louisiana. However, before she
went, she had a Christmas party for the Cherry Grove
children. The food was not exactly traditional holiday
snacks. She prepared a Chinese meal with the help of the
children, Pat Hernandez, and myself. They chopped up
things, and some of the girls would help make cakes from
cake mixes. It was a big deal for them.

The children would range in age from four to sixteen or
seventeen. I don't think we ever got them all still long
enough to count them, but I would say there were usually
about fifty kids running around the house while the food
was being fixed. Of course, we all had to eat with chop
sticks.

Besides eating, we would sing Christmas carols, and
Millie would tell the Christmas story or read it from the
Bible. Sometimes she had a pastor come and talk, but

mostly it was fellowship. We often had a white elephant exchange (each child was to bring a wrapped gift of something old, but still fun or useful). Some of the children wouldn't bring anything, but Millie always managed to provide enough gifts for all to exchange. The children enjoyed decorating her tree if she hadn't gotten to it yet. She had a fresh pine or fir cut from her lot just above the house area. There were always plenty for her, and for any friends who wanted to choose and cut their own tree.

It was a very long party. They started coming at 5:00 p.m. and it often didn't get over until 11:00 p.m. Some of the older kids would stay to help her do the dishes. They all had to be hand washed since she had no dishwasher and she did not use paper. A Chinese dinner on paper bowls and plates? Never!

Millie was very tired and busy Christmas of 1995. She was unable to have the children's Christmas party, but she promised when she got back the children would help her fix and eat a Chinese meal. She did not realize how sick she was. She died before she could get back home.

Now who will tell the children of Cherry Grove about Jesus?

The Old Lovegren House

Almost all of our relatives were very fond of the forest village of Cherry Grove, and of the old Lovegren house. It was "home" to all of us. You can tell how much grandniece, Rachel Evans, loved the place by her description of it. She said,

In the summer of 1994 my sister Amy and I went up to Cherry Grove, Oregon to spend a week with Aunt Millie and to learn something about our Lovegren family history. The Cherry Grove house was the perfect place to do that because, before Aunt Millie lived there, her father and mother had retired from the mission field there. But even before that, this was the family home of my great, great grandparents. Every room had many very

old and some new family pictures, books that were in
Chinese and also books in Swedish, old dishes and old
trunks. Aunt Millie used and preserved the old things.

We stayed in the guest bedroom downstairs. On the
queen-size bed was a down feather comforter, which I
really liked. It was very cozy. The bathroom had an old
deep bathtub that was on foot stands, and the water had a
lot of residue from the old pipes. The floor by the sink
and the toilet was decaying with dry rot. I was very
careful where I stood while brushing my teeth because I
wasn't sure that I might not go through the floor into the
open basement. (The next fall, Millie got this fixed.)

My favorite part of the house was the front closet, or
library, or study, or whatever you want to call it, just to
the right of the telephone and the front door. Walking
into that little room was like walking back into history. I
felt a huge past was there - the land plots of Cherry
Grove, the old account books, some charred from an old
fire, and letters from long ago. My favorite thing in that
room was great grandpa's hat. I now have his hat and I
keep it in my room. Why the hat? I liked it because I
knew it had been on his head, and because it was dirty
and sweaty. I knew a lot of hard work had been done in
that hat. It holds a lot of history and saw a lot of things -
if that hat could only talk of everywhere it went, and
everything that happened while great grandpa was
wearing it!

The kitchen was a bright place with its red-flowered
wallpaper. On the wall over the table were various
beautiful old plates. The sink was ancient. The long
shelves in the old side cupboard contained two or three
sets of dishes; Chinese bowls; lots of glasses but not
many that matched; and odds and ends that dated back to
our great, great grandparents. Of course, she had lots of
chopsticks, but some of the utensils in the drawers were
so old, I didn't know what they were used for. I'm afraid
some of the spices dated back that far, too.

People were always coming to visit her. The phone
would ring, and we would hear Aunt Millie say, "Sure,

come on over." She seemed to know everybody. They often brought food with them and did a lot of the cooking. Their food was delicious, but not the simple kind of things Aunt Millie knew how to fix. When the guests left for home, they thoughtfully would leave not only the prepared food for her, but also spices, packages, and jars for her to use. She often wasn't sure what to do with them. She kept them in case the next guests could use them. So the kitchen had some of the funniest things in it. She had a package of blue cheese in the refrigerator the first year we visited her, and when we came back the next year, it was still there.

Some people stayed with Millie a long time. Niece Emily and her husband, Daniel Thompson, lived with Millie for over a year, and so did Hispanic young missionary, Elizabeth Mendoza and her brother. I decided that if anyone asks me if Millie lives alone, that I would answer, "No - only the faces change." There was usually someone on the beds and couches.

Walking in the laundry room on the back porch was very interesting because of the old tools, hand saws, grass scythes and jars. I don't think Aunt Millie used them. She just left them where they were. It would have been neat if we had a picture of the Cherry Grove house painted on one of those old large saws.

There was a little house shed by the driveway. There were many old things like jars and glassware in the small building. Many old license plates from the thirties and forties hung on the walls. I didn't do a lot of exploring in there because I was a little afraid of the place. It was dark and run down. The garage was even worse. It too had many old implements and license plates on the walls, but it seemed to be ready to fall over. I felt if I slammed the car door too hard, that the whole building would collapse down the hill.

The land outside the old house held as much history as the inside. There were the two little redwood trees that my great grandmother planted that are now forty feet high. The pine seedlings by the road that she planted to protect the land from the dusty traffic are so high and thick that the road is now hidden. Great grandpa liked fruit. His special garden of black cascade berries are still there but wild and snarled. There are apple and cherry trees that he planted. Great Aunt Elva loved flowers. The peonies, irises, lilacs and sweet peas were planted by her. Great Uncle Teon's cedar tree, that he yanked up from the forest and brought home when he was a little boy, now shades the whole west side of the house.

I went back in the oak forest and saw the tree house and the wild cherry trees. I wandered on the overgrown trails and paths of the woods and walked up and down the roads looking at the town hidden among the trees. Aunt Millie showed us the ruins of the Lovegren dam, the first family house in Cherry Grove, the forest road, and lovely Lee Falls.

We visited Birgetta Nixon who wrote a history of Cherry Grove from 1852 to 1977. It is hard to believe that this little town once had several stores, a large lumber mill, schools, and a railroad.

We went to the Cherry Grove Cemetery where Great Grandfather Lee Lovegren and Great Grandmother Ida Lovegren are buried near his sister and brother-in-law, Effie and John Pearson. Another sister, Myrtle, who died from a smallpox vaccination when she was in college, is buried there too. Now even Aunt Millie is resting there.

Amy and I have such wonderful memories of Cherry Grove with its rich family heritage. Yet more important than the place, the history, and even these wonderful relatives, is the faith in Jesus Christ that they gave us (our spiritual heritage), and the sure knowledge that someday we will all meet again in our heavenly home.

Thanksgiving in Cherry Grove

After she retired, Millie spent every Christmas with her sister in California or her brothers either in Georgia or Louisiana. But at

Thanksgiving she stayed in Cherry Grove, and many people came to celebrate the holiday with her - cousins, friends, and foreign students. Cousins Dick and Pauline Chauran said they never knew who would be there, or what kind of food they might bring, or even if they understood what Thanksgiving Day was supposed to celebrate. They remember one year when there were six Oriental students who had never heard of such before.

"What is Thanksgiving?" they asked.

The first year Millie fixed most of the Thanksgiving meal by herself. She got up early to prepare the turkey and get it in the oven in plenty of time. Dick and Pauline came ahead of time to help with the preparations. As the dinner hour approached and the other guests started to arrive, Pauline remarked that they should be able to smell the turkey by now. When she opened the oven for a peek, she was horrified to discover the oven was cold and the turkey still raw! Quickly they surveyed the kitchen supplies, and made a quick change in the menu. Luckily Pauline was a practiced cook, and saved the day for Millie. For her first home-cooked Thanksgiving meal, Millie served Swedish meatballs!

Every year after that someone came to help prepare the meal. Usually, Julie Chauran would come the night before to start the turkey and get things going. Two years, her sister (Carol Chauran) came to fix the turkey, and her parents were amazed. They didn't think she had a clue about how to roast a big bird much less fix dressing and such. Everyone else brought something they had fixed. With so many younger folks willing to help get the food ready, set tables, and do dishes, Millie usually stayed in the living room and visited with guests.

Cousin Linda Pearson said before the meal, Millie would give each person a Bible scripture verse to read, and sometimes she would have everyone stand around the table and tell one thing they were thankful for. Linda felt that made Thanksgiving very special.

Bible School at New Hope

Since there wasn't a Baptist church anymore in Cherry Grove, Millie went to Forest Grove to attend services at the New Hope Baptist Church. She soon became busy in all their activities. Many people close to the church spoke Spanish. They needed a Bible School for Spanish children at their little church and Millie knew who would be great at helping with that project - grandnieces, Rachel and Amy Evans. The girls lived in Texas, but they loved Millie ... and Cherry Grove! Yes, they would come and help! Rachel related this account of their Bible School:

In 1995 Amy and I again returned to Cherry Grove to visit Aunt Millie. She asked us to come and help with a Bible school for Spanish children from a housing project near the New Hope Baptist Church in Forest Grove. We spoke a little Spanish, but Aunt Millie spoke none at all. You may wonder how she could work with so many different groups of people when she didn't know their languages. We found they could tell she cared about them. She used the language of Love.

When we first got there Aunt Millie took us to the Baptist Book Store to pick out the materials we would need for the Bible School in the next week. On the wall of the store was a large poster, advertising a huge Christian weekend rock concert for people in the Northwest. Amy got so excited. She had heard about several of the artists that were to perform, and she liked their music. She said enthusiastically, "Oh, my goodness. Look at the wonderful people who are going to be there!"

The lady in the bookstore told us, "There is no way that you can go, the tickets sold out months ago." But Amy was determined. "I've got to go. I've got to go. I've got to find a way to go," she said.

Aunt Millie started asking around. It turned out that a couple of youth and the pastor from the New Hope

Baptist Church were going to the three-day concert. Amy somehow found a ticket that Aunt Millie helped her pay for, and she rode with Pastor Jim and his group to the concert. They slept in tents, had only cold showers, stood in long lines to get in, but Amy loved it.

Aunt Millie and I drove back and forth to see Amy. We even sat through some concerts. Here was Aunt Millie, this older woman, sitting in this Christian concert with us, listening to hard rock music, and it didn't faze her at all. She just loved being with young people.

In between times, Aunt Millie and I planned the Vacation Bible School, and we passed out fliers telling about the school to the families in the migrant workers' housing project. Two years before, Aunt Millie had young summer missionaries come to help her with a backyard Bible club at the project itself. This time we were to meet at the New Hope Baptist Church, but she had again asked for two summer missionaries who were working with the Baptist Association to come and help us.

Sabrina and another Amy, whom we called Amy K., came to work with us, and they also stayed at Aunt Millie's house. They had the guest bedroom. I slept on a couch that made into a bed in the front room, and Amy slept on the couch in the living room. Aunt Millie slept up in her little attic room. We actually would have been quite comfortable if it hadn't been for all those mosquitoes that thickly hung around the ceilings of that old house. We couldn't seem to get rid of them. I could pull the sheets over my head and still be full of bites.

During the week of Bible school, for a makeshift clown outfit, I dressed up in great grandpa's old hat, his trousers and shirt. I wore one of Aunt Millie's scarves as a tie. I put Vaseline on my face so that white flour would stick on my skin. My poor red lipstick was gone after one week of putting it around my mouth and on my nose. I used eyeliner to make wrinkles around my eyes.

Aunt Millie dropped Amy and me at the housing project to attract the children and have them follow us to the

New Hope Church. I carried Aunt Millie's little tape recorder playing our theme song, and we sang as we walked. I think I still remember it ...

> "There's a trail of treasures right there for us to see,
>> There's a trail of treasures there for you and me,
> If you look you're bound to find
>> Treasures God has left behind.
> Trail of treasures there for us to see
>> Treasures of the Lord."

When we all got to the church, Aunt Millie, the summer missionaries and Amy had the children line up with the American and Christian flags and the Bible carried in the front as they marched into the building. I quickly ran inside to take off grandpa's old clothes and the flour make-up. After some songs were sung, the children were divided into three groups - the really young ones, grades 1-3, and grades 4-6. I worked with the oldest class. Besides the four of us, who were staying with Aunt Millie, we also had helping us two young people from the New Hope Baptist Church and the pastor's wife, Louise Johnson, who had taken a full week off of work to help. We had about forty children each day.

One thing that was surprising to me about Aunt Millie, although she was 75 years old and had a bad leg damaged in a car accident, it was hard for us who were teenagers to keep up with her. By the end of the week we were so tired and worn out.

On Sunday night, we invited the parents to a service to see what the children had learned. We had a good response. They wanted us to stay. After we had gone home to McAllen in South Texas, Aunt Millie worked with others to get a Spanish-speaking church started. The only Spanish speaking pastor in the association agreed to come on Sunday nights to hold services and help them organize a church.

Aunt Millie considered the New Hope Baptist Church her mission field at home. She helped them all she could. Both Jim Johnson, the pastor, and his wife, Louise, had to work to make ends meet. Millie had noticed that they didn't get the support of prayer or fellowship that she had always enjoyed on the mission field. She tried to give them that support.

Millie gave them a lot of encouragement She invited many Chinese students at Pacific University in Forest Grove to attend. Some did, and some were saved, but as the school year drew to an end, they moved away. Everything seemed to be against the church. They were deeply in debt. Often there would only be about ten people on Sunday morning. Yet this small group of people tried to help the Hispanic group all they could. They planned to provide child care Sunday evenings so that the parents could calmly attend the Spanish services.

A young Hispanic missionary came from the South to help with the work. She and her brother stayed at Aunt Millie's house for a year. She used Aunt Millie's car until someone gave her an old one to use. Her brother was still in high school. They stayed with Aunt Millie until she felt too tired to have them, about three months before she died.

There were so few people at the morning services at the New Hope Church that Pastor Jim did everything. He led the singing, he played the piano, and he preached. One time when we were there, Pastor Jim called on Aunt Millie to play the invitation hymn. My sister and I were amazed, "What? Aunt Millie plays the piano too!"

You could tell she hadn't played in a while, but she did very well.

God's Will for New Hope

Louise Johnson, the minister's wife, was so thankful to have Millie in their church. She wrote especially to tell me how much she loved her:

> Millie attended our church, The New Hope Baptist Church of Forest Grove, Oregon. She was dedicated to God and to our church. She drove 24 miles on winding roads to get there even when she was 76 years old. She prayed for our church, and she got others to pray for us too as we went from struggle to struggle. I was the pastor's wife, but she was my guide in many ways. We would sometimes talk until one in the morning. (People who knew Millie well, knew she was a night person. You could call her very late at night, but not before 10:00 in the morning.) She helped me with church books and she was my prayer partner. When I was low, Millie would say, "It's prayer time." We would then have a quiet time together with the Lord.
>
> I would drive her to some of her meetings in her car. When she came to pick me up, before we left my driveway, we would pray for God's mercy for a safe trip. She was a great witness and an example for everyone.
>
> Every Sunday, our little church went out to lunch together and had a great fellowship. She was lovely to the children in the community. Everyone knew her as Aunt Millie.
>
> When she had a car accident, she didn't complain. I knew angels were watching over her. I stayed with her during her rough stay in the hospital. We talked about how God wanted her to slow down. So I helped her to church on Sunday nights driving the beautiful but dangerous country road to her home.
>
> Our church family went to her house at Christmas time. We helped decorate her tree, we sang Christmas carols

and, of course, ate. It was wonderful, and we will all miss that fellowship this holiday season.

We did not know what God had in store. We were shocked and saddened to lose Millie in February. I was even more shocked four months later to lose my husband, Jim, on June 19, 1996, also of lymphoma cancer (Jim was only 50 years old). Because of debts on the parsonage, both it and the church building were sold. (I don't know what happened to the Hispanic group.) Now I try to understand God's will in our closed church, and in the deaths of Jim, my pastor husband, and Millie, my very special friend. Our community will miss both of them deeply. Only God knows the answers.

"And we know that in all things God works for the good of those who love Him, who have been called according to His purpose" (Romans 8:28).

Life's Little Disasters

My daughter, Faith Keller, explained:

Aunt Millie's love of people created interesting situations for anyone fortunate enough to have Millie spend a few days at one's house. Before one knew what was afoot, Millie had invited any number of people over and many were speaking Chinese. On other occasions one might drive for hours to help Millie meet someone or other.

The most disastrous of these experiences for me was when Aunt Millie spent a few days with us in the dead of winter in St. Louis. I had 5 children, aged infant to 8 years. We took off in the early afternoon to drive 2 hours to visit missionary friends who were home on furlough. We had an enjoyable trip asking Aunt Millie questions. As we exited the interstate highway near our destination, we hit an icy patch on the road. The car spun about 100 degrees and hit the guardrail on the bridge over the interstate we'd just exited. As we sat against the guardrail looking down on the traffic below, all we could say was: "Praise the Lord for keeping us on the bridge." The 5 children were startled, but we were all fine. The car, however, did not drive straight. I had to keep the wheel turned in order to drive a straight line. We spotted a lonely garage not far away and eased the car in there and explained the situation. The man sent us all inside to the warmth of his garage and took the car for a test drive. We were all praying! Eventually the man returned, said the car looked fine to him, refused payment of any kind, and off we went with no difficulties! We enjoyed a nice visit with Aunt Millie's friends and left there after the early winter sundown. We were about 1-1/2 hours from home on a lonely strip of interstate when our car ran out of gas! I hiked across a field in the dark to knock on a farmhouse door in hopes they would call a local garage for me. Although there were people inside, noone would answer the door, due, no doubt, to a rash of drive-by shootings in the country at that time. For the same reason, no cars or trucks stopped to help us either. I hiked back across the frozen, stubby field to where my elderly aunt and 5 little ones were shivering in the car. We prayed. A few minutes later a police car pulled onto the shoulder behind our car. He kindly called a gas station to come and bring us enough gas to reach their station and stayed with us until we were safely on our way - actually followed us to the gas station! The policeman commented that for "no good reason" he had decided to alter his usual patrol route that evening. Normally he wouldn't have been on that piece of interstate yet for hours. Aunt Millie and I pooled our funds to buy gas and went on home without further incident. Later, my thoughts were that when one ran around with Aunt Millie one could: A. expect the unusual to happen, and B. expect the Lord to provide.

Millie and the Co-Eds

My younger daughter, Charity Ali, remembered two quick Millie visits. Her comments were:

When I was a freshman at Judson College in Elgin, Illinois, I got a call from Aunt Millie saying she was coming through my area. All she needed was to be picked up from the airport, and then she had a free night to spend with me. Well, I was used to this while living at home. No problem. There were usually two cars to choose from and at least one of us who had the time to go get her. But now, I was away at school, a lowly freshman with no car and no friends with cars. I tried to explain that I couldn't possibly find a way to pick her up from O'Hare Airport. Eventually she called back with a new plan.

She had worked it out with cousin, June Bruce, now residing in Evanston, Illinois, to be her transportation for the weekend. Instead of staying with me at the college, we would both stay with June. After our overnight, we went to some fancy luncheon somewhere in Chicago for Chinese students. At least, that's all I can surmise of it now. I know that I was almost this clueless about it then too. Millie had the uncanny knack of combining visits in such a way that you often weren't sure who you were with and why you were there. (It was a retirement party for a Hong Kong missionary, Stephanie Czechowitz, who worked with boat people.)

When I was a senior in college, Aunt Millie stopped by the Chicago area once again. I don't even remember the transportation situation that time. I just remember that it would turn out to be a visit neither I nor my roommates would ever forget! It was another quick overnight visit. After spending a night on a typical dormitory bed, Millie awakened with a strong desire for coffee. My two roommates and I lived in a little dormitory apartment. We actually had a kitchen. I'm sure that none of us had coffee on hand, so Aunt Millie must have come prepared. She got out one of our sparse kitchen accessories, a small aluminum pan. I guess she decided along the way that she needed a cover to her pan, because a few minutes later her water was boiling and one of our few plates had a large browned, burn spot on it.

A few minutes later when she went in to the living room to open the curtains, a crash was heard and Aunt Millie was bending over something on the floor. I rushed in from the bedroom to find my delicate, ceramic angel laying in pieces. In perfect control, I assured Aunt Millie that it was O.K. and then stole away to the bedroom where I quickly fell apart. That was one of my prize possessions, one of the few really thoughtful gifts given to me by my brother, Jon. My roommate, Cathy, was aghast. She knew the angel had tremendous heart value. The morning passed from there rather uneventfully, and Aunt Millie made her way to another destination - a burned plate and a broken angel left in her wake. When I returned to our apartment that afternoon, I found Cathy bent over a rather sad looking replica of my ceramic angel with her own fingers nearly glued together from all the Elmer's Glue it had taken to do her repairs. No, we would never forget Aunt Millie's visit this time!

Of course, my own mother broke and lost several of Aunt Millie's beautiful things, including hand embroidered silk tapestries and a real tiger rug. It must be a family thing.

Hitting a Deer

Grandniece, Rachel Evans, told about an unusual experience in Oregon,

When we came to visit Aunt Millie in 1994, she planned a trip for Amy and me that included driving up to Canada. I guess we just assumed that there was money available, because she always made it seem like that, but a lot of times there wasn't. The day before we planned to leave, Millie opened a letter with a check for one hundred dollars in it. It was from a friend she hadn't seen in a long time.

"Oh good," she said, "now we can go."

"What? What do you mean, 'Now we can go?'" I asked.

"Well, I was needing a little more money, I just didn't know where it was coming from," was her reply.

That was pretty funny - planning a trip that she couldn't afford to take. (Actually that was not unusual. She assumed, that if it was God's will, He would supply the money for her plans.)

We mainly needed to worry about gas since we were visiting relatives who would feed us and provide lodging. Amy and I were interested in learning more about our family history so we looked forward to meeting cousins in Vancouver and Seattle, visiting a grand old house in Preston, where our great grandfather had lived as a boy and visiting an old cemetery in Fall City, Washington where our great, great grandfather and grandmother are buried.

Before we ever left Oregon, my sister Amy was quizzing us about different states. She had a 50 State Book that told us about state nicknames, flowers, capitals, and other things. Millie and I had some of these things memorized. We were enjoying ourselves and the lovely wooded drive on an unbusy state highway when suddenly a deer darted out in front of us. I don't remember ever seeing the deer, but my sister said I screamed as we hit it. We immediately pulled off to the side of the road, not sure what it was. A gentleman behind us stopped too. He wanted to make sure we were all right, and could drive to the next town. He also pulled the very dead deer off the road for us.

We drove slowly to the next town, hearing an awful squeak every time Millie turned the wheel. The deer had damaged the left front side of the car. Millie seemed calm as she drove to the nearest gas station. The bad squeak was caused by our pushed in fender. We asked several guys if they could help pull it out. They tried but they couldn't and finally they left. I sat there pulling on it while I pushed my foot against the tire, and suddenly it popped out. I thought that was funny, since we had had all those huge guys pulling on it and none could get it out.

Millie found she couldn't open her door. It was jammed shut. Some other fellows on motorcycles helped pry the door open with a crowbar, so that we could get Aunt Millie out. From that point on, she rode in the passenger seat and I drove. It was much easier for me to crawl over from the right seat.

After such an incident most people would have returned home, but not us. We continued on our journey. Everywhere we drove, Aunt Millie wanted to stop at the rest areas to get free coffee and doughnuts. Then because she drank so much coffee we had to stop again to use the restroom. Everywhere we stopped we had guys looking at the car, and telling us their stories of hitting deer, cows, and horses. They said many people had died hitting deer, and we were very lucky that he hadn't turned in such a way as to flip over the car hood into the windshield. We did feel lucky and very thankful.

Cats

Millie liked cats. Cats also liked Millie. Strange cats would usually purr as they rubbed against her legs or jumped into her lap as if they knew they were welcome and would get petted.

Even when Millie was on the mission field, she tried to have a cat. Once in Hong Kong, her cat fell out of her third story window. Millie was horrified. She ran down the stairs to pick up the mangled pieces. He was very scared and shaky but apparently unhurt. Kitty never sat in that window again.

Millie's last cat was the biggest and most spoiled of all. He was huge. It took two arms to carry him and he still hung over either end. He had short gray hair with lots of different markings. She called him Sir Montgomery, Monte for short. The title Sir shows the elevated position he held in her household. She loved the cat, talked to him, and tried to take very good care of him.

The first summer that Rachel and Amy came to visit Millie a veterinarian had convinced her that Monte needed his teeth cleaned because he had too much tartar on them. So they took poor Monte to get his teeth taken care of. Monte was not very cooperative. They drugged the cat before they could clean his teeth. The next day when they came back to pick him up, he was still literally drunk. He was so funny. He leaned on things as he walked around. He swaggered back and forth and then would fall over. Millie just sat and laughed at him, but she also felt sorry for him. He was kind of like her child.

Sir Montgomery got away with a lot of things. He was allowed to sleep on her bed, and he drank from the toilet in the bathroom. When Millie was on one of her many trips, he showed his anger and loneliness by scratching at the wallpaper. He had shredded some of it. He was scolded, but not too seriously. Her kind neighbor, Nadine, always saw to it that Monte had plenty of food and water when she was so often gone. When Millie was home Monte would catch field mice and put them on the back porch to show them off. She didn't like that very much.

After Millie died, Bonnie Evans came up to help straighten things in the house. She asked her daughters, Rachel and Amy, what they might like of Millie's things. Amy immediately said, "Sir Montgomery". Their special cat had died of feline AIDS, but even if it had been practical to take Monte all the way to south Texas, they couldn't. He already had a new home in Forest Grove with a family that is usually home. He seems content and happy.

Aunt Millie Was Our Aunt Millie

When Miss Ruth Pettigrew retired, she decided to stay in
Hong Kong with her Chinese friends where she had spent most of
her adult life. As a young missionary, Millie admired her and
learned many things from her. Many people thought that this
decision to retire in Hong Kong would be Millie's choice, too,
since she also loved the Chinese people so much. She had lived in
the Orient even more of her life than Miss Pettigrew. As she got
older, folks in Hong Kong and Macau asked her about her future
plans, expecting to hear that she intended to stay on the mission
field. But Millie would answer, "I'm not like Miss Pettigrew. I'm
not alone. I have a large family in the United States."

Millie really did have a large family - this is only part of it

How true! She had two brothers, one sister, eleven nieces and nephews, their spouses and children, and many, many cousins. People who only knew her overseas would be surprised at what a family person she was. Among all the other letters she wrote, she took time to write family letters in which she not only explained what she was doing, but also gave tidbit news items of what the rest of us were doing. We kept up with other members of the family through Millie.

When she came home on furlough, she often first came to see me, her sister Edie, or Norman, her brother. She often went the long way home from China so she could visit with brother, August, and his family in Jordan.

She tried to make all special family events - births, graduations, birthdays, weddings, and holidays. She was with me when our daughter Faith was born - in fact, she chose the name Faith when Al and I couldn't decide on a name. At that time, she took care of 16-month-old brother, Mark, and had the "privilege" of potty training him. She learned firsthand how hard it is to take care of little children, and get anything else accomplished.

All of the family members have wonderful memories of our Aunt Millie. Here are a few of them:

> One of my favorite Christmas memories from childhood is the brown package that would always arrive a few days before Christmas. The return address was Macau or Hong Kong, a far-off and magical place where my Aunt Mildred lived and worked as a missionary. Each year wonderful little gifts of ceramic creatures or silk slippers would emerge from the strange dark green or brown cushioning papers. I am certain that Mary and Joseph could not have been more awestruck with their gifts of the Magi than I was each Christmas when that exotic package arrived.

> As I became an adult and a doctor, I became interested in Aunt Millie's two small medicinal balls made of green jade that were good to roll around and stimulate various pressure points in the hand, and Tiger Balm, the ancient

ointment of the Orient that Aunt Millie always carried in her purse. She would offer it to anyone who had various aches or pains. While she was there to share her life and testimony about Jesus, she had incorporated Chinese things into her life.

Edie Lovegren- niece

When I was five or six, I remember seeing Aunt Millie asleep. She slept with her feet straight down in front of her. She looked like a ballerina standing on toe, with no bend at the ankle, and her toes pointed down. As I looked through the blanket, I thought her feet were missing!

During our tour of China in 1993, Aunt Millie and I shared a hotel room most of the way. She was very interested in the comfort of all the others on the tour. When we boarded the boat that would take us on the four-day cruise on the Yangtse River, she was glad to see water in the showers. When everyone was taken care of, she said with her cozy little smile, "I think it's time for some coffee." Aunt Millie was such an avid coffee drinker that she brought along enough for everyone!

Miriam Lanier- niece

When I was a little kid, Millie was visiting and sharing my room. I woke up thinking it was morning because Aunt Millie was puttering around the room. I jumped out of bed and flung the closet doors open, looking for something to wear. I thought I was late for school. Aunt Millie told me it was 2:00 a.m ... she hadn't gone to bed yet! We had a good laugh!

I was amazed at how strong her "Southern" accent was in spite of the fact that she had not lived in the South in so long. Those vowels just went on and on.

I asked her one time, "How do you keep cool when you drink hot tea in the hot climates of Asia?" She smiled and said, "I just sit still and think cool thoughts!"

Linda Rowland - niece

We have two other late night owls in the family: Earl Nelson in Minneapolis, Minnesota, and Bonnie Evans in Texas. When they were up at two or three o'clock, they sometimes called Millie long distance, just to talk. After all, it was only midnight or one in the Pacific time zone. Millie would surely be awake. They were right!

Earl Nelson -cousin

I was near Millie in California one day when she dialed the phone and talked animatedly in Chinese to someone for about five minutes. When I asked who that was, Millie said it was just a wrong number.

Rhonda Lambert - nephew Jon's wife

One day I drove Millie and a Chinese friend to the airport to pick up another Chinese friend. We were going from the terminal to Disneyland. One Chinese friend just spoke Cantonese, the other just Mandarin. And I just spoke English. Millie had to translate everything twice.

Evelyn Lambert - nephew Mark's wife

In 1981, when Angela was about six, she took a recent envelope to school with two lovely stamps. The teacher asked, "Why, Angela, who do you know that lives in Hong Kong?"

Angela replied, "My Aunt Millie, but she really lives in China." Astute in her childlike way!

I would probably never have known about the travels of the disciple, Thomas, or about the Nestorians if Aunt Millie had not been so enthusiastic about them. Her side quirks and interests were definitely a fascinating feature of her personality.

James and his brothers were impressed to learn a few years ago that Aunt Millie was the "Mayor" of Cherry Grove. When we visited in 1989, they were much taken with the town and the opportunities for young boys to explore and roam. All were willing to stay. Millie managed to survive for a week with her house overflowing with 19 Lamberts. She had a little Chinese gift for each one. She shared everything with us - even the flu bug that Hope had brought from Southern California. She applauded the building of the tree house and the opening of the trails. It was such a wonderful time, because she treated all of us as very special people.

Faith Keller - niece

Aunt Millie didn't look like the average older person. She looked sort of Chinese. Various studies say that couples who live together and love each other for a long time begin to look like each other. I think Aunt Millie had an Oriental look because of her intense love for the Chinese people, and her long life living among them.

James Keller - grand nephew

After Aunt Millie's car accident in 1993, she had trouble walking because of the hole in her leg. But that didn't stop her from going with the family to see the tramway at Palm Springs or hiking in the Indian Canyons. She couldn't manage the steep path, but she sat on a bench at the top and talked to people while we hiked.

Timon Keller- grand nephew

Aunt Millie always wanted all members of the family to know each other. She was always trying to get the cousins together. She encouraged me to have a heart for missions and learn all I could about missionaries. One year at the Acteens missions camp, the guest speakers were a missionary family from Hong Kong. I couldn't wait for them to finish their talk so that I could ask them if they knew Aunt Millie. I introduced myself and shyly told them that my aunt was a retired missionary to Hong Kong. They politely asked who that might be, but did not show any enthusiasm. I said that her name was Mildred Lovegren. Their expressions changed to absolute delight, and one of the sons of the family announced, "Why that's my Aunt Millie, too!"

Through Aunt Millie, we seem to have all sorts of missionary cousins. The family explained that in Hong Kong Mildred Lovegren is a great favorite with all the missionary children, and they all call her Aunt Millie.

Angela Kloster - grand niece

The very last group that Aunt Millie spoke to before she entered the hospital for the last time was my group from Texas. She had already had some treatments. I called my grandfather and grandmother, Norman and Viola Lovegren, to let them know that I was in New Orleans. They said that they would come down to see me and bring Aunt Millie, who was visiting them.

When they came to the First Baptist Church building where we were staying, every door was locked. I kept running around trying to find an open door. I knew it was bad for Aunt Millie to walk so much. At last I finally found the one door that was open and then I had to run all around the outside of the church to find them, and lead them back to the unlocked door. It was really neat to see them.

They came right before our worship time and were able to join us as we started singing. Grandmother knew our youth songs and sang along. Grandfather sat and listened, and Aunt Millie was in a real worshipful attitude, very much enjoying worshipping with young people. Then we asked Aunt Millie to speak to us. She told stories about working with youth in Hong Kong and Macau. She talked about how God always provided for her.

You could tell she was very tired then. It was so wonderful to have them with us, but after they left, I just had to sit down and cry because Aunt Millie was so sick. It was my last time to see her and my group was the last group to hear her talk.

Rachel Evan -niece

A Life of Song

We are from a musical family. Our mother played the piano well and had a beautiful voice. When she was younger, she was often asked to sing solos. Papa's family also sang and played instruments; they provided much of the music for their Cherry Grove Baptist Church. Papa still enjoyed singing bass when he was 90 years old. We children were not particularly talented but we all had fun with harmony, and as we grew up, we not only sang at home, but in choirs.

One of Millie's earliest memories in China was going to sleep listening to mother playing the piano with the sound of the river in the background - we lived in the city of Losan where two tributaries of the mighty Yangtze join together. Mother liked hymns and classical music. After she was grown, when Millie heard pieces of music that Mother use to play, the music seemed empty, as if it was missing an important element. It was several years before she realized the music was incomplete because it didn't contain the soothing sounds of the river.

During Millie's first term of service in Southeast China, Papa and Mother were serving in West China. As the communists swept over the country, some missionaries were expelled (Millie), some placed under house arrest (Mother) and some imprisoned (Papa). Mother was released after a year-and-a-half and went to live in British-owned Hong Kong with Millie in her apartment.

We hardly dared hope for Papa's release but after more than four-and-one-half years, Papa was allowed to leave China at the gate in Hong Kong. Mother and Millie were waiting for him. They went to the apartment which was very soon crowded with missionaries, friends of all nationalities, and news reporters asking questions. A missionary friend of Millie's, Dr. Carter Morgan, said, "Amid all the crowds, noise, and confusion, Millie was sitting peacefully at the piano, playing and singing, *To God Be the Glory,* a special favorite of hers."

Millie and I often sang in harmony when we were together. I remember one particularly wonderful evening, when all of our Lambert family were in Cherry Grove with Millie. After the little children were put to bed, we started singing choruses and hymns. Sometimes our daughter, Faith Keller, was at the piano, sometimes our daughter-in-law, Evelyn Lambert, played, and sometimes someone played a guitar for accompaniment. Long after Millie, my husband Al, and I had sung ourselves hoarse, our four children, their spouses, and the two oldest grandchildren continued to sing through Millie's hymnbooks. They didn't stop until after 2:00 AM. A very special time together! Millie often mentioned our night of song.

Millie always encouraged my ragged efforts at playing a piano or guitar by ear. She felt badly that I hadn't received the music lessons that she had, even though this was partly my stubborn fault. When I started writing down music, Millie and our daughter, Faith, were my greatest fans. They encouraged me to teach them the songs and eventually even to get them published. Her favorite song of mine was "God's Love Is Always There".

The last three weeks of Millie's life were very hard for her, and for all of us. Millie had lymphoma. Not only was she often unable to talk, but we weren't sure what she could understand. Several members of our family took turns staying at the hospital with her. We read scriptures and devotionals, and we read the cards that people were sending from all over the world. We also quietly sang. My brother, Norman, and I even tried a chorus of *Jesus Loves Me* in Chinese. It is the only Chinese I know.

One afternoon my sister- in- law, Alta Lee Lovegren, told me that she said, "Mildred, I'm going to sing a song to you. You mustn't tell a soul about this, because everyone knows I can't carry a tune."

Then she sang:

"When He cometh, When He cometh,
      To make up His jewels;
Precious jewels, Precious jewels,
      His loved and His own.
Like the stars of the morning
      His bright crown adorning
They shall shine in their beauty,
      Bright gems for His crown."

When Alta Lee finished she told Mildred, "When our children were very small, your mother told me that she sang that song to her own little children - Mildred, August, Norman and Edith. So I also started singing it to our two young daughters - Miriam and Linda."

She said this pleased Mildred. Her eyes twinkled, and she smiled.

I, Edie, had the late night shift, because I'm naturally a night owl (though Millie could always outlast me). Several nights, Charley and Jo Purvis came to stay the night. How thoughtful! One night in particular when Millie was having trouble breathing, we took turns choosing a hymn and quietly singing it together. Some of the nurses commented about it being nice to hear soft singing. One said she thought Millie was humming along with us. Amazing. She was! From then on, we could sometimes see and hear that this was true.

I'm sure that Millie, now in heaven, is enjoying singing more than ever before. And now our family up there - Papa, Mother, cousins, aunts, uncles, and grandparents - are joining with her in songs of praise and glory to God.